A War of Daisies

The Four Horsewomen of the Apocalypse

Book One

____

A.A. CHAMBERLYNN

For information contact A.A. Chamberlynn at
www.alexiachamberlynn.com

Cover design by Novak Illustration.

ISBN: 9798691192203

To the women who claim their power

There existed no town quieter than Hawk's Hollow. A town of farmers and a town of merchants, a town with a lazy creek meandering through it, a town nestled beneath the shadows of red mountain peaks. It was not the sort of place one might expect to be the spark point of the Apocalypse.

But then, of course, that's why they chose it.

From his vantage point atop one of the skinny buttes jutting up from the valley floor, the demon watched the lights of the town sparkle below him. Night settled across the earth like a blanket, and a fingernail moon dangled high above. He could hear the cicadas in the valley below, thrumming and chirping. He'd go mad if he had to listen to that all night. The earth plane was so…*visceral.* A cool wind scraped across the rock, and the soft whisper of it almost masked the sound of something—someone—landing quietly behind him.

The angel stepped up next to Beziel, his golden wings brushing against the demon's red ones.

"Fancy meeting you here," Beziel said with a wry smile.

"It begins again," Alinar said softly. His skin seemed to soak up the moonlight, emitting a faint glow that encircled them both. "Do you think you can pull it off this time? We won't go quietly."

Beziel smiled again. "Arrogance is one of *our* traits. Watch yourself."

Alinar made a hmmph sound in his throat, barely audible.

"These four… they are special," Beziel said. "Powerful."

Alinar locked the demon in his amethyst gaze. "We will see what side they choose."

From the hills behind them, the lone howl of a coyote broke the stillness. The angel and the demon turned their eyes from each other and back to the quiet town below.

Beziel's words shivered between them. "Well then, old friend, it begins."

CHAPTER ONE

Willow

The afternoon blazed so hot and so bright that Willow was having a hard time taking proper aim, and damn it all, if she missed her shot she would shoot the sun itself out of the sky. Waves of heat rose up from the hard, red earth, covering everything in a haze of watery lines. Sweat dampened the base of her spine, and dust swirled around her boots.

She fired.

The high, sharp sound of glass shattering sounded better than a choir of angels. Her target, a bottle on a log, now lay broken in tiny pieces, a spray of blue across the dirt. Willow's heart skipped a beat and her blood pulsed swiftly in her veins. She lifted the Colt to her lips and kissed it, and the metallic tang in her mouth tasted like victory. Victory and power.

A soft nicker from her mare Bullet alerted her to company. For a moment she didn't see anything, which didn't sit well at all, but then a familiar Appaloosa emerged from the copse of birch trees near the river. Its rider sat bareback, her skin the same cinnamon tone as the mountains rising behind her, her hair ink and midnight. Willow stuck her gun in her belt as they approached.

"You *do* know that no matter how good you are, they aren't going to let you enter the sharpshooting competition or the race." Penelope signaled her gelding to halt and swung off him. She always dismounted face forward by swinging her leg over her horse's neck. "Girls aren't allowed to enter."

"First of all, I'm a woman," Willow said, hips cocked to the side, hands resting on them. "But—" she cut off Penelope's protest— "I'm well aware that women aren't allowed, either. Because Hawk's Hollow is *way* behind the times. It's nearly the 20th century for crying out loud." She stopped there and waited until Penelope pressed for further details.

"So, you're out here shooting your gun for the fun of it?"

Willow's lips twisted into a smirk. "Well, not that that wouldn't be a perfectly legitimate reason, but no. I'm going to enter the competition. I'm just going to do it as a man."

Penelope's brow furrowed. "I'm not following."

"I'm going. To pretend. I'm a *man*," Willow said with great patience and a roll of her green eyes. Sometimes her friends really lacked imagination.

Penelope stared at her for a moment, and then began to laugh. Loudly. The sound of it carried up into the cloudless turquoise sky and bounced from the red peaks surrounding them.

"What's so funny?" Willow narrowed her eyes to dangerous slits.

"You." Penelope waved a hand in Willow's general direction. "You're way too pretty to pull off being a boy. I mean, your hair for starters."

Willow looked down at her waist-length, arrow-straight platinum hair. It was true. The hair had to go. "So, I chop off my hair. And I bind my chest. Easy."

Penelope muttered something under her breath about not having much of a chest to bind, which earned another famous glare. "And what of your mother?" she asked, louder this time.

"I'm technically an adult," Willow began, but then stopped. It was a weak argument, and she knew it. Being an unwed woman and all, it didn't matter that she was legally an adult. Again, antiquated. "But she'll be out of town. Delivering a big shipment all the way to California."

Her mother really couldn't blame her for being as rebellious as she was. After all, she herself was an airship pilot, and Willow's dad was an outlaw. It was like putting together two tigers and expecting a house cat.

A frown tugged at Penelope's lips. "She's going to find out. And she's going to kill you."

"What's life without a little drama?" Willow shrugged, then took two strides to her chestnut mare and swung up into the saddle. The leather creaked softly, her seat and legs melting into it like they were one and the same. She sighed. With a horse beneath her and cold iron strapped to her hip, she didn't need a thing in the whole wide world.

Penelope jumped back up onto her own horse. "Fine. It's your funeral."

"Will you bring flowers?" Willow grinned, then let out a cry and pressed her legs against Bullet's sides. The mare shot out across the earth.

They led for an eighth of a mile, but the Appaloosa wasn't about to let them win. Willow heard hoofbeats behind her as they came up fast. Nothing but flat red earth and blue sky lay before them, blurring like a watercolor painting as they flashed across the plains. Far, far in the distance, mountains waved them on. Out here Willow knew no boundaries; Hawk's Hollow was a dot on a map that held no power over her. Out here she was the sky.

The Appaloosa's nose came into view at her elbow. His chest was flecked with foam, his shoulders dark with sweat.

Penelope laid low across his neck, his black mane mingling with Penelope's own raven locks. The horses drew neck and neck. One nose would surge forward, then the other. Red, black, red, black. An eagle swooped down from above to watch them, flinging its shadow across the parched dirt.

And then it was over, the horses spent and the wind tired of chasing them. Willow reined in Bullet and gave the mare a pat on the neck. She pranced proudly in place.

"I defy any of the men to beat us in a race," Willow said. "We're the fastest thing they'll ever see."

"The race is about endurance, not speed," Penelope pointed out. "Not as much your strong suit."

"That just means it's easier," Willow scoffed.

Penelope raised her eyebrows. "A hundred miles in two days? If you say so."

"I do."

"Well, I'd better get going. I assume you'll be at the fairgrounds tomorrow?"

Willow nodded, eyes aglow. Tomorrow marked two weeks until the Hawk's Hollow Annual Fair, and just about the whole town showed up to see who was signing up for the race, rodeo, and shooting competition, and to watch the try-outs for the team sports. It was almost as big a to-do as the fair itself.

"You're signing up for the rodeo, aren't you?" Willow

asked. Women were allowed to compete in roping, reining, and trick-riding, just not the bronco riding, shooting, or the race.

Penelope shrugged. "Dynah is. And you know how that goes."

"You should do it anyway," Willow said. "Your sister's choices have nothing to do with your own."

A snort. "We'll see." Penelope waved farewell and turned her horse west.

The two racers parted ways. Willow headed back to her house, taking the long route. Hopefully by the time she got there, her mother would already be gone on her trip. If not, there could be questions, or lectures about staying by herself, or offers to have the neighbors come check on her, and none of those things were desirable in the least. The sooner her mother quit worrying about her when she went on trips, the better.

But when Willow got back to the little house nestled between the river and the red buttes, she saw to her dismay that her mother's airship was still perched atop the cliffs overhead. *Blast it all.*

She hid the Colt in a wooden box at the base of a large birch tree, then took her time unsaddling Bullet and cooling her off in the shallows downstream from the house. The water from the mountains was cold as the stars and bit like a rattler. Bullet snorted and shimmied in place as she scooped handfuls of it onto her neck and shoulders. Willow didn't hear her mother approach until she was almost on them, just the shuffle of a boot to alert them to her presence. Her mother never went noticed unless she desired it.

Willow turned. Her mother stopped a couple of feet away, arms crossed over her chest, dagger sheathed in worn leather strung low across her hips. Faded jeans, fringe jacket, suede hat. Around her neck hung her pilot's goggles, their huge, black eyepieces staring at Willow as if they suspected her plan. Her mother was desperately pretty, and they looked exactly alike except that her mother had more than a tint of strawberry in her blonde, a fact that made Willow jealous as hell. But we all have our struggles in life.

"I'm headed out, kid," she said. Her voice was like the rocks in the river, smooth but hard. "No boys, no guns, no booze, and don't forget to feed the chickens."

"Of course, Lyla," Willow said. She never called her mother by any of the maternal nicknames. "I won't play with dynamite, either."

"Always the kidder." Lyla didn't smile when she said it. "Oh, and one more thing. Don't even *think* about getting involved in that race."

Willow had been expecting this, so her face was perfectly smooth and her eyes unblinking as she said, "Yes, Lyla."

Lyla stared at her for a moment and then rocked back on her boots. "Okay, then. I'm off." She turned and headed along the narrow path up the canyon wall to her ship.

Willow waited until the gas tanks in the ship had ignited the flames that flared out the two large hot-air balloons atop the deck; until the ship had risen above the canyon, spooking all the chickens; until the secondary wings had unfolded and the vessel had soared out of sight. Lyla and her rules with it. Then she retrieved her gun, took Bullet to their little ramshackle stable that abutted the cabin, threw her some hay, and went inside to chop off all her hair. She was of half a mind to smoke one of Lyla's cigars while she did it, but then she'd have to spend well-earned money replacing them before she got back, and it just wasn't worth it. They tasted awful anyway.

The cabin was built from small river boulders and boards made from birch and oak. It had a chimney, two tiny bedrooms, and a large kitchen and sitting room. A window in the front lined with brown plaid curtains let in the gurgling song of the river, a song that Willow was fairly certain echoed in her own bloodstream. She was in love with the river and the canyon and the sky and the open plains. But she was also in love with the idea of seeing other rivers, canyons, skies, and plains. Her father was out there somewhere, exploring the world, seeing new things. It chafed at her, just as much as the idea of leaving did. The two opposing yearnings warred inside her every day, some days one taking the lead, the next the other, like wild horses racing.

She sighed, pulled the rusty scissors out of a drawer in the kitchen, and sat down in one of the wooden chairs. Taking a big chunk of her white-blonde hair in one fist, she tucked it inside the open blades of the scissors up near her ear. With a final mournful look at the shining glory of it, she brought the blades together with a sound both terrifying and triumphant.

CHAPTER TWO

Penelope

Penelope always dreamt of wolves. Red ones and gray ones, occasionally a black or a white one. Sometimes a lone wolf, other times a whole pack of them. Eyes like tiny harvest moons, or perhaps with an edge of green the shade of an exotic lime. The dream often spun out beneath a dark, star-pocked sky, though sometimes it was daytime in the dream, a turquoise so bright it hurt. But one thing remained constant. The wolves always called to her. And when they did, she woke up.

She was awake now, and instantly wished she wasn't, because she could hear very adult sounds coming from her mother and stepfather's room. Her sister, Dynah, lay asleep in the bed across the room. The moon streamed in the window, and for just a moment, Penelope thought she caught the fading howl of a wolf off in the hills. A real one, not one of the phantom dream wolves. The sound of it vibrated in her chest and made her shiver: wolves were much less common than coyotes in this area. She swung her legs over the side of the bed and got up.

The window by her bed creaked as she swung it open, the glass cool against her fingers. The crisscross pattern of the wood framing the panes threw a shadow across her floor that looked like the bars of a prison cell. But this cell was open, and the prisoner escaping. She stepped into her boots, grabbed her leather jacket off one of the rough-hewn posts of her bed, and shimmied through the window.

Night wrapped around her, chilly and welcoming. Her boots landed in soft red earth and a bit of sage that her mother had planted a long time ago. Now her mother planted neat rows of bright flowers at the front of the house. Tulips and geraniums and other flora from across the sea. They fit better with her new life and her new husband. Penelope, unfortunately, did not.

She passed by the corral where they kept the horses and moved quickly and silently into the darkness. A few more steps took her into a copse of birch trees. The ground rose rapidly up toward the buttes at the edge of the canyon. At this time of night, the peaks looked black, black against a purple sky. Penelope hunched forward, using her hands to balance as she climbed the steep incline strewn with rocks and boulders. Her muscles warmed up quickly, and her breath came out in little white puffs. Above, the stars in the sky winked at her as she drew closer.

A quarter of an hour later she hauled herself up onto a small bluff. It was no more than a dozen feet across, wedged between two jagged spikes of rock near the rim of the canyon. From one side of the little plateau you could gaze upon the glittering lights of Hawk's Hollow to the east, and to the west, an endless stretch of plains. The wide-open space called to her like the wolves.

Out there, somewhere in the night, her father's tribe slept beneath the same sky. Or perhaps, like her, they couldn't rest. The people that shared half her blood. The people that her mother had tried to erase from her history. Both hers and Penelope's.

Once, many years ago, her mother had spoken of her father. Penelope had been eight at the time. She'd been needling her mother for years to tell her something about him, anything really. Anything would be better than the nothing she'd received her whole life. It had been painfully obvious from an early age that she was different than the rest of the family. Brown skin and black hair to her mother and sister's freckles and red curls. The way her stepfather treated her like a servant. The stares they drew when they went into town.

Questions even remotely skirting the issue of Penelope's father were met with a sharp tone and extra chores. One day, however, when they'd ridden toward town, just the two of them, Penelope's pony had spooked, knocking her to the ground.

She'd gashed her elbow on a rock and cried at the sight of the blood. She remembered the conversation distinctly.

"Stop crying," her mother had said. "It's only a scrape."

"But everyone will see!" she'd wailed.

"It's just blood. No one will care."

"But… but they say my blood is different. Won't they see?"

It was the silly sort of thing that a child confuses in their head. Her mother had gone very still before she'd finally spoken. "Everyone's blood is red, Penelope. What they mean is… your father… your father is from the Navajo Tribe."

"Navajo?"

"Indians," she said briskly. "That's what they mean when they say your blood is different. You're half Indian."

"Where is my father?"

"He died. When you were only a few months old."

Her mother's eyes had a far-off look as she spoke, her tone hushed. Then, she'd stood abruptly and lifted Penelope back onto her pony. And when she'd remounted her own horse, she said, sitting up very straight and shooting Penelope a look that could frost the mountaintops, "We will never speak of this again. Do you understand?"

And they hadn't.

Penelope shivered beneath the night sky. Another howl carried across the plains, and this time it was a coyote. The moon shone brightly, illuminating everything in a soft glow. Willow thought Penelope could just enter the rodeo along with her sister, like a normal person. She didn't know how it was. With the townsfolk. With her own family. Dynah had competed the last five years, but somehow there was always some thinly-veiled excuse from her stepfather for Penelope to watch from the sidelines.

Penelope let out her breath in one long exhale, watching it swirl like tiny spirits. She shifted to face the plains full-on, her back to Hawk's Hollow, pretending for a moment that the town and her family didn't exist. That her limitations didn't exist. Her eyes scanned the open space before her, and movement caught her eye about a quarter mile from the base of the ridge. She sat up straighter, squinting. A wolf, a real one, white like the moon. And behind it, a rider on a horse.

Penelope went still. Even from this distance, she could tell the rider wasn't from Hawk's Hollow. This was no cowboy on a late-night ride. It was one of her tribespeople.

As she watched, the rider stopped and turned to face her. Her skin prickled. Could they see her, sitting atop the butte? Somehow, she knew they could. They stared at each other, the rider and Penelope, for countless minutes. Then the wolf howled, making Penelope flinch, and the rider turned and galloped off into the night.

CHAPTER THREE

Felicity

If music came from the soul, then perhaps Felicity's was missing. Each tug of her fingers on the harp strings resonated within her, vibrated to her core, and echoed back empty. Like calling into an enormous room with no response.

"Put some spirit into it, girl!" her instructor growled.

Across the gleaming wood-paneled parlor, her mother looked up from her knitting with a frown. Felicity closed her eyes and bent her head to the task, but the music came out thin, hollow. Wanting.

Professor Klimten stood, waving a hand at her in disgust. "That's enough for today, Felicity. I'm not sure where your head is this morning, but I do hope you find it again before the performance at church."

"My apologies, Professor," Felicity said, folding her hands in her lap. She could feel their disappointment, both the professor's and her mother's, but all she could summon in return was a swell of relief. The lesson had ended at last.

They left the professor's austere, European-styled house. Felicity's mother walked behind her, her presence like a red-hot brand, and Felicity knew that as soon as they were alone, she was going to get a tongue-lashing. They stepped out onto the professor's porch, which fronted Main Street running through Hawk's Hollow. Horses and buggies and cowboys and merchants flowed back and forth like fish in a river. The noise of the busy town swirled around her and the sun peered down as if it were judging her, too.

Her mother stayed silent, maintaining a lady-like appearance, as she tightened the sunbonnet that Felicity had already fastened quite adequately around her chin. The silence grew exponentially, building by the second. Silence as they mounted their horses, side-saddle of course. Silence as they wove through the traffic on the streets, and silence as they passed the church, even though here Felicity could feel the weight of that silence the most. Silence until they reached the big white house at the end of the nicest street in town and took the horses into the stable out back.

When the trip finally ended, her mother's scorpion tongue spewed venom. "What is *wrong* with you?" Her anger hurled into Felicity, a near-physical force.

"I was doing my best, Mama…"

Felicity's mother made the sign of the cross over her chest. "God help us if that's true. I will *not* have a daughter that displays her failure in front of the whole town."

"The whole town doesn't attend church," Felicity said.

"Everyone who matters does."

Felicity opened her mouth to start apologizing; she knew she should have done that initially. But her mother had become a torrential downpour and there was no stopping her.

"We've worked *so* hard for where we are, for our business, for this house, for the things you have. So hard. You *know* how much harder we have to work than everyone else, because of who we are. And all we ask is a few simple things. Music is how we praise, Felicity. The harp is your connection to the divine. It shows everyone that you are favored. And you are favored, but you just *squander* it." Her mother's riding crop hit the side of the barn with a loud *thwap,* making Felicity jump.

"Yes, Mama, I understand," she murmured, over and over, but it was another quarter-hour before her mother abruptly stopped her assault, turned on her heel, and stalked into the house.

Felicity took several deep inhales and exhales to calm herself, then with shaking hands she began to attend to the horses. Hers and her mother's both, since of course her mother had stormed off. It was fine, though, she told herself. She didn't want her mother here, anyhow. The barn was her place, the only place she could *breathe.*

It was a quintessential barn, precisely as a barn should be. Strong, wooden beams. Cobwebs here and there. The smell of pine shavings and sweet, fresh hay. Shafts of sunlight shooting down between the rafters. And of course, the occupants. She took the saddles and bridles off the horses and put them up in their tack room, then led each horse to their stall. She brushed them down and made sure they had water, checked their hooves for rocks. She patted her horse Music on her black shoulder and snuck her a sugar cube.

After Felicity had taken care of the horses, she climbed the wooden ladder at the north end of the barn aisle, up into the loft where they kept the hay. In the far corner of the hayloft, she wiggled between the stacks of baled hay, then reached her fingers into a narrow crack between two boards. She pulled out a leather-bound book, along with a small well of ink.

She couldn't help but glance over her shoulder to make sure she was alone. Every time she touched her book, her pulse raced just a little. Slowly, she retreated out from between the rows of hay and sat down on the floor, her back against the bales. With fingers that trembled, but for an entirely different reason now, Felicity opened the book and picked up the feather pen tucked inside.

Ebony scrawlings crisscrossed the pages. She flipped through to the spot where she'd left off. Just the smell of paper and ink made her feel like a normal person again. With these tools in her hands, she was just Felicity. Not Felicity the future harp virtuoso. Not Felicity the churchgoer. Not Felicity the doting daughter of the wealthiest merchants in town. Not Felicity the only girl with brown skin to go to her private school. Not Felicity who had to be perfect all the time because her mother had given her everything, and *why couldn't she just be more grateful?*

She took a deep breath and dipped her pen in the ink. *Just Felicity.* She laid pen to paper.

CHAPTER FOUR

Dynah

A strange thing, beauty. It made lots of people love you, and it made lots of people hate you. And it didn't seem there was a whole lot of in-between, at least not that Dynah had ever seen.

"What about this one?" asked her mother, holding up a bolt of plaid lavender cotton.

They stood in the haberdashery looking at the fabric that had recently arrived from Denver. Her mother held the lavender cloth up against Dynah's chest, and they looked in the mirror across from them. The pale purple made her flame-colored curls pop out like a winter sunset.

"Ooh, that's nice," Dynah said. "Though the blue one is, too." She ran her fingers over a different bolt of fabric, crisp and new. She could almost smell the indigo dye.

"We should get both, I think," her mother said, flashing a hundred-watt smile. Everyone said Dynah got her smile from her mama. That, along with her freckles and bright red hair.

They went to the register and paid for a large piece of cloth in each color, her mother carefully counting several coins and laying them one, two, three on the slick wood counter. Dynah knew the store was owned by the black family, but she never saw them here. The store clerk smiled shyly at Dynah until her mother cleared her throat. He slid the coins into the register with an embarrassed blush. Dynah threw him a huge smile which made the blush reach new depths of color, and they left the store, exiting into the late-morning sun.

With the Hawk's Hollow Annual Fair coming up, Dynah was, naturally, the favorite to win Rodeo Queen. She'd just turned eighteen and was finally eligible. She'd been told for years she was the prettiest thing to walk the earth in these parts, though she had to admit a couple of the other girls gave her a run for the money. As things heated up to the big event, she had lots of boys vying for her attention, hoping to stand by her side as she was crowned a local celebrity. That, and plenty of girls shooting her the stink eye and wishing she'd drop dead.

Her sister, of course, was always at the top of that list, though perhaps for different reasons.

They climbed into their small one-horse wagon and rolled down the dusty street. The haberdashery had been their last stop after picking up horse feed, groceries, and a couple things from the general store. Boys waved at Dynah as she rode by. Once or twice, a grown man stopped and stared as well, which drew an evil look from her mother, and whatever woman happened to be at the man's elbow. Dynah just smiled and waved. Love or hate. She was used to it.

When they got home, her mother drove the wagon around to the back of the house. "Now, you'd better go get changed and head to the fairgrounds for registration," she said to Dynah as she started to unhitch their palomino gelding.

Dynah nodded and headed into the house while her mother finished handling the cart horse. Within a few minutes, she'd changed into a yellow blouse and let her hair out of its braid. It now cascaded down one shoulder. She grabbed her suede cowgirl hat, wiped a few spots of dust off her boots, and headed back out to the barn.

Her horse Moon stood in a small corral next to the barn. True to his name, he was a pale gray from head to toe. He'd been a gift from her parents a few months back, when she'd started training for the rodeo. They performed a variety of roping tricks. Nothing with real steer—that was for the men— but lassoing barrels and such. Moon loved to show off almost as much as she did.

Dynah saddled him up and bid farewell to her mother before riding back toward town. The registrations and tryouts took place on the far side, at the Hawk's Hollow fairground. They held most public events there. There was a large riding arena dead center with several corrals adjacent to it, and a large stage at one end.

She alternated between trotting and loping Moon the three miles to the grounds, nothing too strenuous. It wouldn't do at all to show up sweaty and dusty. She could hear the crowd gathered by the arena almost before she could see it. Pretty much every able-bodied man in town, plus a number of spectators, along with all the local merchants, their wares set out on tables or in the backs of wagons.

There were also bound to be lots of out-of-towners: Hawk's Hollow was the largest town in fifty miles and the annual fair drew a big crowd. Dynah's heart beat faster at the thought. She'd had her eye on a couple handsome cowboys from around here, but wouldn't it be even better if she snagged herself a fine man from Grand Junction or Denver? Someone from money who could buy her a big ranch? Several of her friends were already married, and she could feel the clock ticking on her window of opportunity. She had no doubt she'd find a husband; it was simply a matter of ensuring she found the best one.

As she rode up, she sat straighter in her saddle. Heads began to turn, eyes began to widen, and she just smiled. She knew the effect she had, riding up with her flame-colored hair on her pale horse, belt buckle and saddle gleaming. She was already their Rodeo Queen and they all knew it.

"Dynah!" someone yelled, followed by a chorus of whistles and hoots.

Billy Boynton. Top contender for future husband if Dynah *did* pick a man from Hawk's Hollow. Blonde hair, blue eyes. Almost too pretty to be a cowboy, but those rough, calloused hands told the truth of his upbringing. He was in line to inherit his father's ranch and 3,000 head of cattle. Dynah turned Moon and headed in his direction.

As she sidled Moon in between Billy and his friends, who were lined up on their horses to watch the bronco team tryouts, she threw him a smile. "Hey, Billy."

"How's my girl?" He reached out and tugged at one of her curls. He had a smile that could almost match hers in luminosity. Almost.

"Well I'm fine, now that I'm here." She shot him a look from beneath her lashes.

"They're just starting the bronco team tryouts. You get signed up for the roping competition yet?"

"Not yet."

Billy shrugged. "Everyone knows you'll win anyway."

Dynah smiled coyly and didn't reply. She caught sight of her sister Penelope on the far side of the bronco pen, and they cast each other indifferent nods of acknowledgment. Inside the fence, a tough-as-nails mustang with murder in his eyes stared out across the crowd, sensing the souls of the men who would try to ride him. For just a moment, Dynah considered what it would be like to sit astride him. But no. She knew her place, and that wasn't it. That was for the men.

A loud voice boomed across the crowd. "Who's first?"

Several cowboys jumped up to the fence, dangling atop it like dusty grasshoppers. From behind her came the sound of galloping hooves. Dynah turned to see a chestnut mare barreling through the crowd. The mare looked a bit familiar, but she shook it off a moment later. The tall, lanky cowboy riding her was definitely a stranger. Short, white-blonde hair. A face that needed a proper washing. Eyelashes that would make any girl jealous.

Dynah's attention was pulled away from the newcomer as a weathered man hopped down into the ring and began to warily approach the mustang. The bronco tryouts had officially begun.

CHAPTER FIVE

Willow

A thick crowd had gathered at the arena by the time Willow approached, which was exactly the situation she'd been trying to avoid. Usually, she would have loved to draw the attention her way and show the boys a thing or two, but it was not the time for that. She couldn't afford to stand out, to draw more than a passing glance. She needed to register for the race and the shooting competition and get out of here before anyone recognized her, chopped hair or no.

But there was nothing to be done for it since Sadie the rogue chicken had made her blasted late. She dismounted and tied Bullet to one of the fence posts, then made her way toward the registration line. To her left, people were clustered around the bronco pen for the team tryouts. She preferred to fly solo, which was why she was sticking to the race and the sharpshooting competition. Plus, those were the ones with the big-money prizes. Her ticket out of here.

Willow slowed her step as she approached the cowboys in line, mellowed her swagger. Forced her breathing to slow, shoved a strand of platinum hair behind her ear as she tipped her hat even lower over her forehead, shadowing her face. She'd rubbed some dust on her cheeks to help, too.

The line ran along a fence across from the bronco pen. She got into it and leaned against the rail, casual as a summer picnic. The men around her shot her only the slightest sideways glances before turning their gazes back to the spectacle within the ring. A huge thunderstorm of a horse stood dead center of the corral. It wasn't just his dark-gray coloring, but his eyes, his energy. Everything about that horse was one crack of the heavens away from a downpour of the worst kind.

A man approached the mustang warily. He had charcoal hair like the horse, a weathered and wiry man seasoned by the desert. This clearly wasn't the first wild horse he'd handled. He had a thick coil of rope in his hands, and he rubbed one thumb back and forth across the texture of it. That was the only tell of his nervousness. At least the only one Willow could see. But if she'd noticed that, the horse had noticed infinitely more. They could sense even a drop of fear comin' out of your pores.

Quick as a snake, the wiry cowboy tossed his rope out and looped it around the mustang's neck. The mustang reared and yanked the cowboy off the ground like a ragdoll. Another man ran out and threw a rope around his neck, and then a third, at which point it seemed to Willow they were just ganging up on the poor horse. As they did their best to hold the lunging, leaping stallion in place, someone else ran out and threw a saddle on his back. The bridle was next, which took three more men and a substantial amount of bruising (for the cowboys). By the time they were done, the mustang had hellfire in his eyes.

"Who's on first?" one of the men called.

Willow's body involuntarily twitched toward the ring. She could show these boys a thing or two about taming mustangs. Emphasis on taming, and not the manhandling that had just occurred. But she was here for the race. *Blend in. Don't make a spectacle*, she thought.

"You wanna give him a go?" came a voice next to her.

Willow turned to her left. She hadn't even noticed the man who'd gotten in line behind her. When their eyes met, the breath in her lungs escaped in one big rush.

He was maybe a year older than her. Tall and lean like one of the trees that grew along the canyon slopes. Hair of midnight, eyes blue-gray like the river. His jeans hugged his hips in a way that made her want to bite her lip. And so tan he looked like he'd bathed in river mud. He most certainly wasn't from around here.

"Uh, I'm here to register for the race and the sharpshooting," she managed. She realized she sounded breathy and tried to deepen it toward the end. *Damn it all.*

"A bit young, eh?" His voice was playful and had a slight drawl that felt like chords of music up her spine.

"You're one to talk." Willow planted her feet and crossed her arms over her chest, which felt weird with it bound so tightly.

A flash of something moved over the man's face, but then he smiled. "You're not from around here, are you?"

"I was thinking the same thing about you," Willow countered.

She noticed, much to her chagrin, that several men ahead of them in line had turned around.

The cowboy grinned and raised his hands in a placating gesture. He waved her forward, as if she wasn't already in line ahead of him. "By all means, the more the merrier in a race like this. Though I dare say, you may be the daintiest cowboy I ever did see."

Willow froze, and the cowboys surrounding them went silent. Watching. She could hear hoofbeats and cheers from the ring, but those closest were all waiting with bated breath for her reaction. There was only one thing that could be done.

Willow spun around and punched the beautiful stranger in the face.

His head whipped back, but he didn't fall. When he straightened, she could see blood dripping from his lip. Her knuckles burned, but she held her fist tightly at her side and bit down on the pain. The cowboy's river-blue eyes sparkled, and a smile played over his lips.

"I take it back," he said softly. "You're tougher than you look, cowboy."

Around them, the watchers let out a collective release of breath and went back to their business. Willow turned her back on the ridiculously good-looking cowboy and faced resolutely ahead. There were only eight men in line ahead of her. Then she was home free.

It felt like those blue eyes were burning into her, and it took utmost self-control not to fidget. Why couldn't he just watch the bronco riding like everyone else? When she finally got up the courage to pivot part way and start watching again herself, she saw that he was. Maybe she'd imagined his gaze the whole time. The line dwindled. Soon there were only five men ahead of her, then two. Finally, she stood at the head of the line. "I'd like to register for the race and the sharpshooting."

"Name?" asked the stocky cowboy at the registration table. He eyed her, lingering on her face for what seemed a very long time.

For a heartbeat, her mind went blank. Luckily, there was one fairly obvious choice. "Will," she blurted.

"Will…?"

Shit. She hadn't thought of a last name, either. "Bullet," she spat.

He raised his brows. "Will Bullet?"

She nodded.

"Birthdate? Minimum age is fifteen," he added, eyeing her

again.

That part was easy enough, she'd actually just turned eighteen. "May 5ᵗʰ, 1876."

"Horse's name?"

Double shit. "Um, Bullet."

"Bullet? The same as your last name?"

Behind her, she heard the handsome cowboy snicker.

"Yes, that's correct." She stared at him unwaveringly until he sighed and looked away.

"That's a dollar and a half." He held out a weathered palm for her money.

It was a lot of money, but she'd saved up for it working at different farms here and there. She pulled a handful of nickels and dimes from her pocket and counted them out, trying not to look too mournful over their loss. She consoled herself with the fact that she'd soon have *fifty* dollars when she won the race.

"Alright, Will Bullet riding Bullet. You're registered." The cowboy scribbled her name on a receipt, splashing ink across the page, and handed it over.

Grasping the receipt tightly in her hand (around the edges so as not to smear the ink), Willow stepped out of line. She'd done it. She'd fooled them all. And she'd soon be the first woman to run—and win—the endurance race.

CHAPTER SIX

Penelope

Penelope tried her best not to watch her sister preening across the bronco pen, but it wasn't an easy task. Dynah's laughter bubbled up into the sky every few moments as all the boys (and men) fawned over her. A carefree laugh, the laugh of someone supremely confident in their position in life. The laugh of someone who had never seen a day of hardship. The laugh of someone who had always been loved and adored.

They couldn't be more opposite if they'd tried.

As Dynah turned this way and that in the saddle, her teeth and spurs flashing brightly, Penelope wondered, not for the first time, what her life would have been like if she and Dynah had the same father. How it would feel not to be looked down upon, whispered about, shoved aside, both metaphorically and literally.

Their mother and Dynah's father gave Dynah everything she ever wanted, Moon being a perfect example. Why had Dynah been given Moon? Penelope had never even been allowed to compete as her sister had, let alone getting a new horse just so she could claim the title of Rodeo Queen the year she turned eighteen.

It came over her then, that familiar wave of emptiness and envy. It always felt a bit like a disease spreading through her blood. Her sister felt so very sure that the title of Rodeo Queen was already within her grasp. And all Penelope wanted in the world at this very moment was to ensure she didn't get it. A truth she felt ashamed of, but a truth, nonetheless.

Dynah was never outright mean to her like her stepfather was. But the indifference bit like a bullet. That way of acting like Penelope wasn't *really* part of the family. All three of them acted that way. As if she were some child they'd found on the street. Never once did Dynah acknowledge that she got everything while Penelope got nothing. Sometimes Penelope felt invisible in her own home.

The crack of a gunshot made Penelope flinch: one of the cowboys on the far side of the arena, practicing for the shooting competition. She wondered if Willow had managed to get registered. Penelope had seen her come galloping up on her mare, but they'd of course had to pretend not to recognize each other. The disguise and all.

Another gunshot went off, and Penelope realized the

cowboys weren't practicing. Not exactly. Three Navajo men approached, one on a paint horse, and two on black horses. They rode bareback, in suede breeches and boots. The cowboys weren't aiming at the tribesmen, but they were making a show of things for sure. The crowd went quiet.

The three riders rode calmly into the crowd, ignoring their antics. They approached the registration table.

"We would like to enter the race," said one of the riders. The other two stayed quiet, their faces emotionless.

The two men sitting at the registration table looked at each other and then back to the Navajo men. "We don't allow in'juns in the race, fellows."

"It is a race across open lands," said the tribesman.

"They're not open to you," said the first cowboy.

"You've got your reservation," the other added. "We suggest you be gettin' back to it."

The Navajo man who had spoken set a small leather bag of coins down on the table. "We can pay the fee. Three entries. A bigger purse for the winner."

"You heard us," said the first cowboy. "Your money ain't good here."

"Afraid of a little competition?" someone called from a few feet away. "I say let them race."

It was Willow, of course. Drawing attention to herself as usual. But now was most certainly not the time, not unless she wanted her cover blown. Penelope felt a flush of admiration for her friend. She wanted to step forward and say something, too, but the words died in her throat. In their eyes, she was an *in'jun*, too. What good would it do?

"You pipe down," one of the cowboys snarled at Willow. "You're lucky I gave you a ticket to begin with."

"You weren't sad to take my money," she shot back.

The tribesman turned to Willow. Their eyes met, chocolate and pale green, and he nodded to her. "Thank you, friend. But we will not stay where we are not welcome."

"It's a shame," Willow said, casting a burning gaze on the cowboys. "It's nearly the 20th century and these boys can't play fair."

"I've had just about enough of your sass," one of the cowboys said threateningly.

The Navajo turned to leave, riding their horses back out through the crowd, which parted like the Red Sea.

When they drew parallel to Penelope, the rider in the back, who was much younger than the other two, cast his gaze her way. Their eyes locked. She could see him take in her skin and hair. Skin and hair that looked like his, though her skin was just a bit paler. He stopped his horse, and the other two did as well. Words passed between them, but Penelope couldn't hear what they said. The crowd watched them watch each other.

And then they turned and rode off.

She belonged to no one.

CHAPTER SEVEN

Felicity

From her seat behind a table of wares from their various shops, Felicity watched the Navajo men stare at the girl. All the merchants had come out for the fair registration day, so she was here with her mother, their wagon loaded with shiny new saddles and suede hats and scarves for the women. Rock candy and ribbons and carefully crafted fiddles. An array of goods to tempt any passersby.

But due to the spectacle unfolding across the arena, no one paid them the least bit of attention.

Felicity felt the girl's shame in her own heart. She knew it all too well, the feeling of being judged for the color of your skin. The girl—she didn't know her name—was fatherless, and her mother had a second husband and a second daughter. Everyone knew the story because everyone knew the second daughter.

Dynah Johnston, future Rodeo Queen. Prettiest girl in town.

And then the tense moment passed, and the Navajo men rode off across the dusty plains beyond the town.

"I don't know how that girl's family deals with her," Felicity's mother whispered tersely. Her hands busily smoothed out non-existent wrinkles in a stack of colorful bandanas.

Felicity turned to face her mother. "Deals with her?"

"Being a half-blood!" Her mother's face puckered as if she'd bitten into a chili pepper.

The irony of the words felt like a slap in Felicity's face. How could her mother say that about someone else who faced the same discrimination they did? But she knew the answer. Her family wanted nothing more than to fit in. Bent over backwards to be just like the other residents of Hawk's Hollow. They earned enough money, certainly. More than most. But what they desired was something money could never buy. A hunger that could never be quenched. Not when they were trying to be a part of a community that didn't want them in return.

The feeling of suffocation rose, as it often did, building, building, building…

A horseless stagecoach rolled up to the edge of the crowd, emitting a blast of steam from one of the many chrome pipes that powered it. Polished mahogany, red and gold paint. The first steam-coach had been built in Denver the year before, and Felicity's father was already working an angle to distribute them down south in their corner of the state. Heads turned as a group of wealthy residents stepped out of the cabin. A couple moved toward their table. Felicity's mother immediately went into full molasses mode. That's what Felicity called it. Thick, sticky, overly sweet.

Air rushed back into her lungs. Not just breath, but wind. It was really picking up all of a sudden. Felicity smacked her hands down on the pile of scarves as a gust swept down from the sky. A row of black clouds rolled toward the arena like a herd of galloping horses. Hadn't it been cloudless just a few minutes ago? Felicity grabbed her straw hat to keep it from flying away, tightening the blue ribbon under her chin. But as she did, the top half of the stack of bandanas fluttered away in the breeze.

"Oh, my!" she heard her mother gasp demurely.

If only these wealthy customers knew what would happen to her if she lost their merchandise. Felicity dashed after the escaped bandanas. It was hard to move quickly in her ankle-length skirt and the tight corset crushing her lungs. Not to mention the impractical heel on her boots, which her mother insisted all the ladies wore. The colorful bandanas were like a rainbow flung across the earth. They'd be ruined within moments if she didn't catch them.

So intent was her focus that she nearly ran into a chestnut mare.

"Hey, watch it!" yelled the young cowboy holding the mare's reins. His voice seemed high for a man, his hair a dazzling shade of white blonde.

Felicity watched in panic as the bandanas rolled between the mare's legs. She half-reared, whether from the flying cloth or the wild wind, Felicity didn't know. She realized that the scene around her had devolved to chaos in a matter of moments. The wind tipping things over, cowboys trying to calm spooked horses, dust blasting into everyone.

Two other horses entered her line of sight, a pale gray and an Appaloosa. She realized with a start that it was Dynah and her half-sister. How they'd gotten here, she didn't know. With the wind blowing sand into everyone's eyes, she could barely see a thing.

Then, though she wouldn't have thought it possible, the wind intensified. A cyclone formed around the four of them, forcing them even closer together. They stood in the bullseye of a small tunnel of wind. A wall of dust and debris surrounded them, rising high into the sky above.

She caught the panicked gazes of the other three. The pale green of the blonde cowboy, the sharp cornflower of Dynah, the dark depths of the Navajo girl. The horses had their heads tucked down; backs hunched up. Felicity couldn't see a thing beyond the tornado that had trapped them.

A rumble, from both the sky and the earth it seemed, and a flash. A bolt of lightning hit the ground between them. The horses whinnied and reared, the glow of it flashing around them. Felicity felt a searing heat wash over her. A zap of energy entered her solar plexus, rocketing up through her ribcage. For a moment, she tasted the night sky. No, not the sky, but beyond. Something further than the sky.

And then, just like that, the cyclone vanished, and the clouds began to roll away. Felicity looked at the others, and they stared back, wide-eyed and speechless. What had just happened? How were they alive?

She heard a scream, and her mother ran up to her, raking her hands down Felicity's body as if she didn't think she was really there.

"I'm okay, Mama," she murmured. Her body felt sluggish, numb.

The crowd swirled in, approaching them with varying levels of disbelief and awe. Felicity and the other three were pushed apart as everyone jostled to get a look at them.

"That was some twister," said one of the cowboys with a whistle.

"Lucky you folks are alive," said another.

And so on and so forth, another two dozen similar comments. Felicity realized, even through her shock, that no one had mentioned the lightning bolt. After several minutes, as things began to die down and people began to return to their business, she started to wonder: had she imagined it in her panic? Surely, they never could have survived such a thing.

She didn't say anything as her mother took her back to their wagon, sat her down, and packed up their wares without her. Before long, her mother had climbed aboard, and they were headed back toward their house. Felicity turned it over and over again in her mind. Everything had happened so quickly.

As they made the final turn for home a few minutes later, Felicity realized that her numbness was wearing off a bit. A fine tremor moved through her limbs. It felt as if she'd swallowed some of that lightning whole and it was bouncing around inside her abdomen, rushing through her veins. Looking down at her trembling hands, for just the barest of moments, she swore she saw a sparkle of light shimmy around her fingers. But when she blinked, it was gone.

She shook her head. That couldn't be possible. Could it?

CHAPTER EIGHT

Dynah

They say a girl needs her beauty sleep, and Dynah most certainly hadn't gotten it last night.

First, her mother had been all over her when they got home. She'd seen the storm clouds roll in from a distance and been worried sick until Dynah and Penelope came back. Her parents had made her tell every detail of the events down at the arena. And she'd shared them. Until the part at the very end.

Because Dynah wasn't really sure what happened in the dust storm. It had come on so fast, and with so much dirt flying around, she hadn't seen much. As she started to describe it to her parents, Penelope, who had been in the other room, began to pass through to go back outside. Her sister had paused, and their eyes had met. And Dynah skipped the part about the lightning and wrapped up her story. As she did, Penelope let the door slam shut behind her.

She'd felt exhausted when she crawled beneath her soft cotton sheets, and she'd quickly fallen into a deep sleep. But rest she did not. Instead, she dreamed. Dreams unlike any she'd ever had before. She didn't remember them exactly. Just darkness and bones and things that wriggled in dirt and flesh. *Not* the kind of dreams that the Rodeo Queen should be having. Dynah had woken again and again, but each time she drifted back off, the strange dreams returned.

And that's how she'd arrived into the harsh light of day: tired, sore, and with dark rings underneath her eyes. Even scarier than the nightmares. Dynah's mother dabbed rosewater on her skin to help with the color, and after breakfast, she saddled Moon and rode toward the arena. She traveled through the birch forests and fields near their homestead on the west side of Hawk's Hollow. Drank in the scent of the steam-plows churning up fresh dirt at her neighbor's farm. Savored the last cool crispness of morning, knowing the sun would soon devour it.

Now that registration day had passed, it was less than two weeks until the fair, and that meant all the serious contenders began to practice publicly. An intimidation tactic, mostly. Show off before the competition, have everyone quaking in their boots come the big day. This marked Dynah's sixth year competing, so normally it would have been old hat to her. Except this was her first time competing with Moon, and this was her first attempt at the title of Rodeo Queen.

Within minutes of arriving at the arena, it became clear that they were not going to be intimidating anyone today. Moon was jittery, practically spooking at his own shadow every five minutes, which was very unlike him. Yesterday there'd been a far larger crowd, and he'd been fine. Dynah became increasingly tense, which in turn only made Moon more anxious. Finally, after about the dozenth jump and bolt, Dynah decided to take a break.

She led Moon out of the arena around to one of the big water troughs, casting a forced smile at two other girls entering the ring. Moon shoved his nose into the trough and drank thirstily, splashing her with droplets of water which she winced away from. The last thing she needed was a ruined blouse, too.

Dynah could feel the dust from the arena settling on her sweaty skin. After watching Moon drink his fill, she realized she was parched, too. Taking a quick look around to make sure no one could see her, she scooped a handful of the trough water to her lips. The warm liquid tasted of earth and metal, but she gulped it down.

From her current vantage point, Dynah could see Hawk's Hollow's tiny train station to the south, no more than a plank platform next to the tracks. Come next week, this whole area would be packed with traveling merchants. The annual fair drew a big crowd of Colorado residents, as well as travelers from other states. Those who wanted to watch the famous endurance race, or maybe even catch a glimpse of a few Navajo, the reservation being so close and all.

A breeze blew down from the mountains to the northeast, and Dynah closed her eyes in pleasure. There were few things in the world finer than the perfection of a cool wind on a hot day after you've been riding. She felt it play over her skin, slide under her curls. Beside her, Moon snorted and sighed. So, they hadn't had the best day of practice. But they still had plenty of time before the rodeo. Dynah patted Moon's shoulder and slowly opened her eyes.

And realized she had an audience.

The black merchants' daughter, one of the ones who'd been caught in the cyclone with her, stood a few dozen yards away on the walkway in front of the hotel. The building closest to the arena, at the far southern end of Main Street. She didn't know the girl's name, only that she was staring at her. That much she could tell, even from this distance.

When the girl realized she'd been caught, she ducked her head and hastily stepped into the hotel entrance. Though she needn't have bothered. Dynah was quite used to being stared at by men and women alike. She laughed under her breath and gave Moon another pat on the shoulder. "Want to give it another go, boy?"

She turned Moon around and came face to face with three of the gnarliest-looking cowboys she'd ever seen. Bloodshot eyes, crooked teeth (where they had them at all), and the whole lot of them in dire need of a bath.

"You'kin give me a go if ya like," one of them said in a raspy voice.

The other two let out a hoot and a cackle, like a pair of coyotes. Dynah's mouth fell open. These men clearly weren't from around here. That was simply not the way one spoke to ladies in Hawk's Hollow, let alone Dynah Johnston.

"I kin show ya somethin' else strong 'tween ya legs," growled a second man. His eyes looked more than bloodshot, they almost seemed to be… *glowing*. Hungry.

She found her voice. "Excuse me! I have to be going."

The cowboys stood between her and the arena entrance. She attempted to go around, but they moved with her, blocking her passage.

"Stick around, sweet thang," cooed one of the men.

The others leered at her. "We 'ave something' you'll like… promise."

"I said, *excuse me*! I am trying to get to the arena!" Dynah snapped. "Leave me alone."

"Don' be like that… we just wanna be friends wicha."

One stayed in front of her while the other two moved around to each side, effectively blocking her from anything but moving backward. Moon snorted and pranced, his eyes rolling. The cowboy closest to her reached out a grubby hand. His fingernails were so long, they almost looked like claws…

"Stop!" she shrieked, throwing a hand out to shield herself.

The cowboy stopped. His red eyes bulged, and his dagger-like fingers dropped to his side. He coughed, and it sounded wet. The cough turned into a gurgle, and his skin purpled as he began to choke. He raised both hands to his throat as if he couldn't breathe.

Dynah gasped and stepped back as the cowboy fell to the ground. She swung up onto Moon in one fluid movement and spun him for Main Street. Horror and confusion rose in her chest as she fled.

She didn't look back as she galloped through the center of town.

CHAPTER NINE

Willow

The gun shop landed on the list of Willow's favorite places in the whole world. Not the fancy one up on the north side of Hawk's Hollow near the wealthy neighborhoods. But the little hole-in-the-wall down Scarlet Street off Main. More of an alley than a street, really. The gun shop and the smithy were the only stores down here, run by two brothers. Two brothers who knew Willow quite well.

"Why'd ya go chop off yer hair?" Harvey called the moment she stepped foot inside.

A sprawling, open-air shop, it looked more like a barn than a storefront. The forge, a massive stone structure taller than Willow, stood in a covered dirt stall adjacent to the room where the guns and other finished products lay on tables and shelves, up a set of steps away from the blazing coals. Luckily, no one else was there, other than his brother Jonas. Willow raised a finger to her lips and made a hissing sound.

A deep, throaty chuckle rose from Jonas, who stood at the forge, muscles gleaming with sweat from under his tunic. "Isn't it obvious, brother? She's trying to enter the competition in a couple weeks."

Harvey wrinkled his brow. "Girls are allowed to enter the rodeo, aren't they?"

Jonas looked over at Willow from beneath huge, bushy black eyebrows. "It ain't the rodeo our Willow is keen to enter."

Willow felt a swell of something suspiciously similar to affection. It felt nice to be seen. To be *known*. She quickly brushed aside the emotion. Luckily, these two were the only ones in town who paid any attention to her whatsoever. No one else would notice that a lanky cowboy had replaced the girl with the outlaw daddy.

"I trust you two will keep my secret," she said, drawing herself up in an attempt to look intimidating.

Jonas chuckled again. He was six and a half feet tall, at least, with arms almost as big around as barrels. "Sure thing… Will."

"That's actually the name I used in the race," Willow said. She stepped up to the top of the stairs, and a waft of intense heat from the forge blew into her face.

"Clever," Jonas said dryly.

She made a harrumph sound in her throat and approached the closest table of shiny metal objects.

"What's clever abo' that?" Harvey called as he carted buckets of scrap metal over to the forge for Jonas to melt down. "Oh," he said a few moments later. "I get it now."

Jonas grinned and winked at Willow. "What're you looking for today?"

"Just looking," she responded. "I don't have any money to spend."

"Well, let us know if you need anything." Jonas bent his head and began hammering on a piece of metal laid across his anvil, something that looked like it might become a dagger. Orange sparks flew into the air around him, falling harmlessly on his thick leather apron.

Willow nodded, eyes gleaming as they roved over the latest inventory. Jonas clearly trusted her a great deal to turn his back with all this firepower right under her nose…but the brothers were some of the only decent people in this backwoods town. She'd never steal from them.

Beneath the loud clinking and clanking from Jonas's hammer, Willow caught the soft whir of wings in the corner of the shop. She strode over to the far side, furthest from the forge and the entrance, to see the latest gadgets that Harvey had built. One wouldn't guess it from engaging him in conversation, but Willow knew he had a creative brain. She marveled at the tiny clockwork owls, steam-powered dragonflies, and even a brass rooster that somehow sensed the coming sunrise. There were larger birds, too, clockwork hawks and eagles that could deliver messages faster than the Pony Express. The guns still owned her heart, but these came in a close second.

Willow had just turned her attention back to a table of weapons when she heard a voice over her shoulder.

"Getting an upgrade before the competition?"

She spun. People didn't usually sneak up on her. She'd learned how to be quiet—and how to listen—from her mother. Her eyes widened. It was the mysterious stranger from the arena yesterday. He wore a dark blue plaid shirt that made his eyes pop. Damn, he was pretty. But far more importantly, how had he gotten the drop on her?

"I'm happy with the iron I've got." Willow patted the gun at her hip.

The cowboy peeked down. His gaze felt hot on her skin—men didn't tend to stare at a woman's hips in public. But then, he didn't know she was a woman. "Colt Army Model? 1860?"

"Uh, yeah. Good eye." She didn't know what else to say, so she studied the guns intently. In fact, she'd made of point of ignoring boys her whole life, and she didn't see a reason to stop now. Her fingers absentmindedly brushed over the cold barrel and smooth wooden grip of the closest one.

"Colt Dragoon," the cowboy said. Even his voice was beautiful. Velvety and dark, a rush of raven wings.

"I know," Willow said, trying not to sound snappish. Both because he was right, and because his allure had started to really get on her nerves. "Have you ever shot one?"

He nodded. "Not my favorite."

"Heavy as hell, that's for sure."

She moved down the long table of weapons, eyes and fingers searching like a truffle pig for just the right thing. The cowboy stuck with her every step of the way. He seemed to be standing awfully close, so close she could feel the heat of his body wash into her. It made her head all fuzzy, which was not at *all* what she needed right now.

"Smith and Wesson Model 3," she said, her hand resting on one of the pistols. "I used to have one of these."

The cowboy flicked his gaze to hers. "What happened to it?"

"Lost it in a bet," she said, a low whistle escaping her teeth. "A sad day."

"I can imagine."

He stopped moving, and Willow instinctively stopped, too, like there was a line connecting them. "Now *this* is an interesting gun."

Pale gold, with a tiny barrel, rings that formed a knuckle duster, and a short knife at the end. "An Apache Revolver," Willow whispered in reverence. "It must be a new arrival. I've never seen one before, but I've read about them."

The cowboy cocked his head to the side. "A sharpshooter who reads?"

"Well, don't you?"

A chuckle. "I suppose I do."

Willow picked up the Apache gingerly, sliding her fingers

into the knuckle rings. She turned and pointed it across the room, squinting one eye slightly to sight her invisible target.

"It's not much for distance," the cowboy said. "But at close range? Not half bad."

"You've shot one before?"

He nodded. "May I?"

The cowboy reached out and slid the Apache off her fingers. As he did, their fingers touched, and a pulse of heat ran up her arm. Willow was very much aware of how close they were standing. For several long moments, she forgot she was supposed to be pretending to be a man. Which reminded her that the cowboy thought she *was* a man. Which probably meant that the sparks she felt flying between them were, in fact, only flying one way. She tried not to feel too deflated. Perhaps men always stood this close to one another? The secret life of the male of the species.

The cowboy lifted the Apache, turning it this way and that to admire its delicate construct. "A beauty, that's for sure," he said, looking at her as he said it. Willow felt another wave of heat, and this time it had nothing to do with the forge.

A sudden commotion outside broke the moment. A horse galloped down Main Street, and a group of a half-dozen cowboys, who had most definitely just come from the saloon, sauntered (stumbled, really) onto the side street. Willow sighed. She loved everything about the annual fair. Except the influx of annoying visitors from out of town. The drunken cowboys stumbled inside the entrance to the shop.

"Well, what 'ave we 'ere?" whistled one of them.

"Looks like acoupla squeaky clean saplins' with no weatherin' at all," said another, pointing at Willow and the handsome cowboy. "You two run on down to the toy store, ya hear? Guns are for real men."

"And I suppose you think that's you?" Willow said, crossing her arms over her chest and widening her stance. "Jonas! You're gonna need to mop one of these boys off the floor in a minute."

"Callin' fer backup, little'n?"

"Hardly," Willow scoffed.

"Take it from me, gents," the handsome cowboy said, "This one here packs a mean punch. He may not look like much, but he breathes fire."

"I think I'd liketa see that," one of the newcomers said.

"Me, too!" chorused the rest of the group.

Jonas emerged from behind the forge, wiping soot from his hands onto his apron. "Gentlemen. Public intoxication is not permitted in Hawk's Hollow. Go sleep it off before someone calls the Sheriff."

Harvey emerged behind his brother, crossing his arms over his chest.

"Cert'n'ly," said the one who had started all the talk. "After we see the little fire-breather, 'ere."

"I hardly think you're in any condition to fight me," Willow growled.

Her eyes scanned for a way out, but the group entirely blocked the entrance to the shop, and most of the narrow street beyond. Not that she was planning on running from a fight. But her odds weren't so good.

"Boy, you so skinny I could blow ya over wit' one big huff," one of the men said, roaring with laughter.

Willow felt a heat building in her chest. Pure energy, surging into her. Like the lightning that had struck during the cyclone the day before. She didn't believe in miracles, but something had kept her alive. Kept all of them alive.

And that same feeling coursed through her veins now. Rawness. Light. *Power.*

"I've never seen such a pathetic lot of men in my life," Willow said. "If I were you, I'd look to the company I kept." She swept a disdainful look over them all, felt that heat radiate toward the drunken cowboys.

They followed her gaze and began eyeing each other. The next moment, insults began to fly back and forth faster than bullets. Voices rose, chests puffed out. Then a punch flew, and the next thing Willow knew, the cowboys were brawling in the dirt.

"I'll go get the Sheriff," Jonas said with a sigh, jogging around the heap of men.

Harvey just stared wide-eyed, mouth agape, looking from Willow to the pile of men and back again. Willow stared, too, the scene before them so surreal she almost didn't believe her eyes.

"Come on," the beautiful stranger said. "Let's get out of here before they come to their senses."

They skirted around the brawlers, and soon were back out on Main Street.

"Well, that was certainly interesting," the cowboy said, shooting Willow a look.

"Yeah." Her brow wrinkled. "Remind me never to drink. What a bunch of imbeciles." A horrible thought crossed her mind. "Do you think those guys will be in the race?"

The cowboy shrugged. "Probably. In it for the prize money. Rule breakers who'll do anything to win. You better watch yourself."

"Well, you'll need to watch yourself, too," Willow said, a warning in her tone.

"I'll be too far in the lead to worry about those lowlifes." He grinned.

"But behind me, of course."

The cowboy tilted his hat back, appraising her. "Perhaps. Tell you what."

"What?"

"We can watch each other's backs. Until the final stretch of the race, that is." His gaze burned into hers. "Then it's every man for himself."

"An alliance? Interesting." Willow leaned back against a wooden post, returning the penetrating look. "What's your name, cowboy?"

"Zane," he said, and there was that feeling once again of music up her spine.

"Well, Zane," she said. "You have yourself a deal."

CHAPTER TEN

Penelope

I'm entering the rodeo," Penelope announced at dinner.

Silence fell around the table.

Her mother went still and looked down at her steak and potatoes, as if not acknowledging it made it cease to be. Dynah's mouth hung open, a forkful of food halfway to her mouth. And her stepfather slowly went from pink to red to purple.

"A little late, don't you think, girl? If you think for one second we have money to pull together at the last second—" His voice went from a low growl to a high shriek like a train whistle.

"I don't," Penelope said. "I'll pay for it myself."

"And how're you gonna do that?"

"I've been working here and there." Penelope shrugged.

"Helping unload shipments at the feed store. Doing some cleaning at the hotel."

Dynah's fork clattered back to her plate. "What exactly are you going to enter in the rodeo?"

"Trick riding." Penelope raised her eyes to meet Dynah's. "Don't worry, sister, I won't be competing against you."

"Well," Dynah scoffed. "Moon and I have been practicing for months."

"So have I," Penelope said softly. "Not that anyone bothered to ask."

"Penelope," her mother started, finally looking up.

"Now, listen here, you ingrate!" Her stepfather boomed. "I'm not sure what you're gettin' at, but we provide you with everything you need!"

"Absolutely, Roy," Penelope said. She stood up from the table quite calmly. "You treat me and Dynah completely equally."

And she walked out the front door of the house.

More silence, for several long moments, and then an explosion of noise as her stepfather went ballistic. Shouting and the sound of dishes breaking. Penelope didn't know where her wash of courage had come from, but it fled as Roy whipped open the door and began to storm after her.

"Get back here! Penelope!"

She had a hundred-foot head start on him, and she was light of foot. Could probably outrun him. But then another wave of heat rose inside her, devouring her fear. She didn't know where it came from. All she knew was that she felt *angry*. Angier than she'd felt in her whole life, everything she'd suppressed for all these years rising within her like a grizzly bear. Penelope spun to face her stepfather. It wasn't like it would be the first time he'd hit her.

Roy almost had flames coming off him as he approached. "You think you're gonna talk to me like that at my *own* table?" he spat. "You're lucky you didn't go to the orphanage the first day I set eyes on you."

Her mouth opened of its own accord. "A gift for your bride to be?"

"I forbid you to enter that rodeo, you hear me?" Rage spouted out of him, black and thick. "You need to learn your place, and I'll be damned if I'm gonna have a rude little Indian girl running around my house. Now come 'ere."

"Why?" she snarled.

"Because I'm not done with you!" Spittle flew out of his mouth as he advanced on her.

Penelope raised her hand then, palm out toward her stepfather. Later, she wasn't quite sure why she did it. He was too far away still to strike her. But whatever the reason, she lifted her hand, and she thought *no*.

Roy stopped in his tracks and let out a cough as if a fly had gone down his throat. Then another, and another.

And Penelope turned and walked off into the twilight

without a backwards glance.

A few minutes later she sat astride Domino. She skirted south around the birch forest and out into the open fields. She planned to loop down around Hawk's Hollow to Willow's house in the southeast. But as she rode, the desert plains came into view to the west, and she found herself drifting toward them. That pulse in her blood, that *pull* in her blood. A call waiting to be answered.

A wolf howled, and then, far in the distance, she saw him again. The lone rider, the one she'd seen the other night from atop the butte. A blot of ink against the sliver of sun setting on the horizon. She didn't even try to imagine how he could be here, now, after what had happened back at the homestead.

Penelope turned Domino and headed out into the open plains.

CHAPTER ELEVEN

Felicity

Felicity escaped to the barn as soon as she'd finished dinner. She didn't know what she would do if she didn't have these brief bits of time to herself. Everywhere else she went, she went under her mother's watchful gaze. The house. The store. Her music tutor. Church. It was simply improper for an unmarried young lady such as herself to leave the house without a parent, her mother said. Lord knows the things that could happen. And worse, the things people would say.

It'd been three days since the dust storm at the arena, but it seemed an eternity. She still felt a blaze of energy running through her. And she didn't even know what to think of the light she'd seen shimmering out of her hands. She must have been in shock. That was the only logical explanation.

Felicity wished she'd gotten a chance to talk to the other girls (not the fair-haired cowboy, she'd never talk to a man alone) after the storm. But what would she say to them? She didn't know any of them. Well, she knew who Dynah was, but everyone did. That didn't mean Dynah knew her.

An ache of longing tightened her chest.

She'd spotted Dynah earlier in the day when she went to borrow some lamp oil from the hotel next to her family's millinery shop. Her mother had actually let her walk next door by herself. That's when she'd caught a glimpse of that flame-red hair. It burned a shade of red unlike any other.

Felicity had stopped to watch Dynah practice for just a moment, and then had seen a group of nasty-looking cowboys approach her. It had been clear, even from a distance, that they were not a pleasant sort. As they'd circled Dynah, Felicity had begun to wonder if she'd need to call Sheriff Longford. But then Dynah had swung up on her horse and galloped away.

Beautiful, even in flight.

By that time, of course, her mother had noticed her absence and had come to look for her, which earned her a string of chastisements. The day had gone downhill from there. As Felicity and her mother made the rounds, checking on their store clerks, cross-referencing ledgers, picking up money, checking the stock of supplies before the annual fair, they'd discovered that a group of vagrants had been stealing from the haberdashery. Which had put her mother in a ripe mood for the rest of the day. Aside from being the center of unwanted gossip, there was nothing her mother hated more than losing money.

This had somehow led to Felicity needing to do extra harp practice and extra prayers for the day. When she'd finally finished that, along with household chores and dinner, she was exhausted.

Out in the barn, she groomed the horses for a bit, and spoiled Music with extra carrots. She'd had the mare for about five years, since her father had shipped her in from Kentucky. A Thoroughbred in a land of Quarter Horses. They were both fish out of water in this place. But it made a statement, and her parents did *love* to make a statement. It had made Felicity uncomfortable at first and gave people yet another reason to stare at her as she rode about town, but Music had soon become her only friend. She had no one else to talk to.

So, Felicity told Music about the cyclone and the lightning and the strange light she thought she saw coming off her hands. And Music listened, with a twitch of an ear here and a snort of understanding there, and an occasional wiggle of her velvety nose across Felicity's arm. Well, the last part was likely a search for more carrots.

Afterward, Felicity climbed into the hayloft to get out her book. Inspiration rose strong within her. Ink flew across paper, her pen making a steady scritch-scratch sound against the ivory pages. It soon stained the tips of her fingers, but she ignored it. She could wash that off later.

In her story, there were no white houses encircled by white picket fences. No harps. No church (this part made her insides quake with guilt). And no parents. Instead, there were girls with blue eyes and flaming hair. Or, rather, one particular girl.

Usually, her cheeks flamed as she wrote. If ever her mother found this book… the horror of it was too great to contemplate. It was Felicity's greatest danger and the air she breathed, both at the same time. She couldn't *not* write it. But it was so, so wrong. At least, that's what the church would say.

Tonight, however, whatever spirit moved within her moved freely. Confidently. The story unfolded without limitation, without the judgments of her own mind. The heat she'd been feeling since that lightning strike grew and grew and grew inside her. Felicity lost all sense of time as the story consumed her. She bowed willingly beneath the altar of this creative force, and it was the truest form of worship she'd ever experienced.

And then a flicker of light spun off her hands.

Felicity squealed and dropped her book and pen. Her book fell into the vial of ink at her side, tipping its contents into the hay. This time she shrieked. She scrambled to pull her book out of the pool of ink before it was ruined, and to right the overturned bottle before every last drop vanished. Ink was expensive. She'd barely gotten away with sneaking this one into the barn as it was. Tears pricked the corners of her eyes as she tried, to no avail, to wipe the huge smear of ink off the words she'd just written. Some of her best words ever, gone in an instant. Along with most of her ink.

A creaking sound below directed her attention away from her predicament. Had her mother come to check on her? Or her father?

Panicked, Felicity stuffed the book, the pen, and the vial of ink back into their hiding spot. She covered the ink-stained hay with fresh hay and hastily tiptoed to the top of the ladder. From there, she peeked down into the barn to see who it was.

The door to the tack room stood open, but she couldn't see anyone. After a moment's debate, she climbed quickly down the ladder. The soft cadence of voices drifted up the barn aisle. Felicity cocked her head. It didn't sound like her parents. But if it wasn't them, then…

A woman stepped out of the tack room, her arms laden with a saddle and several bridles. Farther down the aisleway, a man led Music out of her stall. She snorted and pranced, eyes wide.

One look at their dirty faces and tattered clothing told Felicity all she needed to know: these people were stealing from her family. Her family, who worked so hard for everything, who were always trying to keep up with the other townspeople. Her family, who was always looked down on, despite everything they did. And worse, they were trying to steal her best and only friend.

"Unhand my horse!"

Felicity realized that the words spoken in a cold, commanding voice were her own. They'd come out of her mouth unbidden. She felt as surprised as the expressions on the faces of both thieves.

They turned to flee.

"How dare you!" she screamed.

The woman dropped the saddle but kept the bridles which she had flung around both shoulders. The man dropped Music's lead rope. They ran out the other end of the barn, and Felicity found herself chasing them. She didn't know where this rage inside of her came, but it boiled hotter than the lightning.

She followed the thieves to the fence at the back of the property, where they had loosened a couple of boards. As they tried to slip through, Felicity shrieked again. "Thieves! You don't know the meaning of *true* hunger!"

That white glow shot off her hands again, and she shook her fists at them. The man looked at her, eyes huge, and shoved his partner through the gap in the fence.

"Felicity!"

Her mother and father came running out of the house. "What's going on?" her father asked in a stern voice.

"I caught two people stealing our tack from the barn! And they tried to take Music!"

"Stealing?" Her mother placed a hand over her heart and looked as if she might faint. "Harold, the same ones from the store, you think?"

Her father's forehead wrinkled in consternation. "It seems likely. A mighty big coincidence, otherwise."

"We need to call the Sheriff," said her mother. "Oh, what will the neighbors think?" She fanned herself with her free hand to indicate how close she was to swooning to the ground.

"It's not our fault we had thieves!" Felicity said indignantly.

Her mother straightened somewhat. "We need to manage the story, is all. If the neighbors just see the Sheriff here without knowing why, the rumors will spread faster than wildfire. By then it will be too late."

Felicity's father ignored his wife's antics. "I'll go fetch the Sheriff."

"I'll go 'round to the neighbors," her mother said. "Tell them what happened. Just need to go freshen up first. You should come with me," she said to Felicity. "Tell everyone what you saw. How frightened you were." Her mother began to walk back toward the house.

Felicity ran to put Music back in her stall. She caught up to her mother at the steps of their massive wrap-around porch. Ostentatious white columns towered over them. "I wasn't frightened. I was angry."

Her mother didn't say anything. Felicity wasn't sure she had even registered the words. "Go change into the pale blue dress. White bonnet. And—" She cut off with a gasp.

"What is it?"

"Your hands, girl!"

For one horrifying moment, Felicity thought her hands were glowing again. But when she looked down, she realized what her mother had seen.

Ink.

"How on earth did you get so much ink on your hands?!"

"Um, I had a spill earlier."

"In the barn?"

"Of course not!" Felicity took a deep breath, though her heart raced. "Before that."

"Why didn't you wash up properly?" Her mother started fanning herself again. "Go, Felicity. Now. You will not disgrace this family."

As Felicity turned and headed toward the washroom, she realized two things: first, her mother was more concerned with reputation than the fact that someone had trespassed on their property and stolen from them. And second, neither of her parents had once asked if she was okay.

CHAPTER TWELVE

Dynah

To say that things were tense inside the Johnston residence would be a grave understatement.

Dynah didn't think she'd ever seen her father as furious as he had been after Penelope mouthed off and stormed out of the house. He'd always had a temper—it seemed most men did—but his mood that night made the fires of hell seem mild in comparison. She and her mother tried to stay out of the way as he stomped around the house, knocking things over and kicking the dog when it got in his way.

To make matters worse, it seemed he'd developed a nasty illness. In between shouting at Dynah and her mother (especially her mother, for birthing such a disgusting creature as Penelope, for defiling herself with an Indian man), he'd been taken with bouts of coughing so intense they doubled him over. Which only made him angrier. Which made him yell more. Which made him cough more.

Dynah had been sure she was in for another sleepless night, but shortly before midnight, her father had gotten so weak he couldn't get out of bed. She felt intense relief, followed quickly by severe guilt. With a pillow over her head, she managed to sleep despite the sounds of coughing in the next room.

The next morning, Penelope was still gone, and her mother sent Dynah into town to fetch the doctor. She saddled up Moon and headed east, out of the birch forest and red buttes toward Hawk's Hollow. Usually, she made the trip in a leisurely half-hour, making sure to arrive fresh-faced and with hair perfectly windblown. Today was not such a day. Today she galloped, giving Moon only short trot breaks in between.

When she arrived in town, she looked a hot mess, quite literally. Covered in sweat and dust, hair in a tangle. Moon's nostrils flared in and out, and when she pulled him up outside the doctor's office on Main Street, he hung his head wearily. She tied her reins to the rail outside and ran up the steps.

"Miss Johnston! What's the matter?" asked Helena, the doctor's office assistant, as Dynah threw open the door.

"My father has taken ill," Dynah said. "He's been coughing all night. Can't get out of bed."

Helena's face wrinkled in concern. "Let me go get Dr. Hudson." She got up from her desk and headed into the back room where the doctor saw patients, her plaid petticoat swishing behind her.

Dynah took a seat in a leather-back chair and waited. The front room was sparsely decorated, just a large bookshelf on one wall, holding all manner of medical texts and periodicals, the desk, two chairs for customers, and Dr. Hudson's medical degree framed on the back wall. Dynah's eyes wandered every surface, looking for something, anything, to distract her.

She still couldn't believe Penelope had up and left like that last night. Where did she think she was going to go? Who would take her in? She loved her sister, but the townspeople only tolerated her unfortunate blood because of their mother. She'd end up having to come back home and take her punishment from Dynah's father. The longer she was gone, the worse that punishment would be, of that, Dynah had no doubt. She cringed to think of it.

Dynah and her mother had been on the receiving end of that punishment from time to time as well, but Penelope had it the worst. When her father got in one of his moods, the best thing you could do was just stay quiet and do as you were told. Usually Penelope did that, too. Dynah couldn't imagine what had come over her last night, to speak to him as she did. And somewhere deep inside, just for a moment, a tiny part of her had been proud of her sister. A part that Dynah had quickly shoved down. Hopefully, Penelope had gone to Willow's house. She didn't have the energy to worry about her sister and her father at the same time.

The door to the back room opened, and Helena emerged, followed by Dr. Hudson. They could have been brother and sister, though Dynah knew they weren't. Both had wispy blonde hair, brown eyes, and pale skin. The doctor, however, rose tall and thin, whereas Helena was shorter and full-figured. For an older woman, she drew a lot of attention from the men of the town. Dynah made a point to notice these things.

She noticed none of these things now, however, as Dr. Hudson strode toward her. Because instead, she saw a strange black shadow that hugged the frame of his body. It startled her so much that she gasped, hand flying to her mouth.

"Oh, there, there," Dr. Hudson said soothingly. "I know you're distraught about your father. Try not to worry, my dear, at least until I've taken a look at him."

Dynah bowed her head and nodded as he patted her back. With her gaze turned toward the floor and her curls falling like a curtain to shield her face, Dynah could only see the doctor's feet. The brown leather of his shoes, gleaming slightly. The cuff of his pants. The dark, shifting fog encircling him.

It clung tightly to his body, moving and swirling slowly as if alive. Dynah realized after a moment, much to her horror, that it emitted a faint whisper as well. A sound that evoked the nightmares she'd had since the day of the cyclone. Of things that crept in the darkest of places.

After a moment, Dr. Hudson straightened. "I'll get my horse from around back."

He walked off, and Dynah let out a sigh of relief.

"You take care now, Miss Johnston," Helena said. "He'll fix your father up in no time."

Dynah nodded numbly and walked out to collect Moon. She tried to compose herself as she untied his reins from the rail with shaky hands. Was she having hallucinations? Perhaps because of the stress; first Penelope, now her father. Sensing her upset, Moon turned his head and nudged her with his soft nose. Dynah patted him on the neck distractedly and swung up into the saddle.

"Ready?" Dr. Hudson asked as he rode around the corner on his bay gelding.

Dynah nodded, trying not to tremble. She blinked her eyes several times, but the shifting shadow surrounding the doctor remained.

She led the way home, riding alongside the man and the writhing darkness.

CHAPTER THIRTEEN

Willow

Bullet flew across the earth so quickly that Willow felt sure at any moment they'd sprout wings and rise into the sky. She lay low across her neck, red mane whipping in her face. Heat rising up from the mare's pumping muscles, heat rising up from the plains. They were speed incarnate. They were unstoppable.

After about a mile Willow reined her in, and they trotted the next mile to cool off. When they reached the curve of the railroad tracks where they swooped south past Hawk's Hollow, Willow knew they were getting close to home. She'd been doing sprints with trot intervals in between to build up their endurance for weeks now. Lately she'd increased the distance, going a dozen miles each day, south out of the canyons by her house until she reached the wide-open sprawl of the plains and then back again.

The cross-country endurance race would last two days and cover a hundred miles. From Hawk's Hollow south along the Navajo reservation border, up to Devil's Eye Peak, and back along the mountains to the north. One big circle back to town. A grueling test of horse and rider. Dangerous terrain. Hot temperatures. Snakes, mountain lions, and coyotes. Willow grinned at the thought of it.

In addition to being a woman, she also had another secret weapon she bet none of the men had: Bullet was a mustang. Willow had found her out in the plains three years prior, alone and injured, and had nursed her back to health, sleeping in the barn with her for a week straight. Along the way she'd earned the mare's trust, and it hadn't been long before they'd been galloping across the open plains. Mustangs had the trifecta of speed, endurance, and hardiness that made them perfect for this sort of race. Their meeting had clearly been meant to be. And soon they'd be out of this place, exploring the world together.

As she came within sight of the red rock canyons again, and the glittering curl of the river leading to her house, Willow saw another rider ahead. A rider with tan skin, black hair, and a golden buckskin. Her heart climbed into her mouth.

"Zane," she called when they got within distance. She slowed Bullet to a walk. "What are you doing out here?"

"Same thing you're doing." He smiled. "Practicing for the race. Except I have a disadvantage—I'm not from around here, remember?"

"Well, the race is going to be held that way." Willow raised a brow and pointed to the west.

"Eh, we've been all over today. Just winding down." He reached down and patted his gelding on the neck. The buckskin snorted and pranced in place.

"Where'd you say you were from again?"

A grin. "I didn't."

Willow wasn't going to let him dodge so easily. "So?"

"I don't call any particular place home." He shrugged. "And you, Will? You've lived in Hawk's Hollow your whole life?"

Willow rolled her eyes. "Yeah. Unfortunately."

"Why is that unfortunate?"

"Let's just say Hawk's Hollow is a bit behind the times." Willow sighed. "I want to see other places. Like you have."

Zane pulled his gelding alongside Bullet, riding so close their knees brushed against one another. "Don't underestimate a place to call home," he said softly.

Willow looked over at him, and for a moment his gaze was distant, as if he saw something other than their surroundings.

"Well," she said. "I can always come back. After I've seen a few things."

"So, is that your plan if you win the race? Use the winnings to get out of here?"

Willow nodded. "Yeah."

"Well, then, it will give me sorrow to beat you."

His grin was back, and she almost reached out to swat at him playfully before remembering that men didn't do that to each other. *Don't flirt, you moron!* It was exceedingly hard to remember to be a man while in Zane's presence. Damn it to hell. If he blew her cover...

"We'll see about that. I hope your walk is as big as your talk."

"Oh, it most certainly is." His voice deepened, and the look he shot her gave her heart palpitations.

"Um, well, I was about to head home. I'm sure I'll see you around." Willow turned Bullet toward the river.

"I'm sure you will," Zane said.

As she rode away, Willow wanted to kick herself. She'd never been interested in boys. Why now? It was the worst possible timing. She needed to win this race. Then she'd not only have the prize money, but she'd also reveal to all the antiquated townsfolk of Hawk's Hollow that they'd been beaten by a woman. They'd have to change the rules going forward. It would be her farewell gift to the place she'd grown up.

Zane, however, was not part of her plan. His presence was dangerous. If she lost this thing because she felt giddy over a handsome cowboy, she would never forgive herself. She made up her mind then and there: no more Zane. Not until after the race started. They had their little bargain, and she'd keep up her end. But until then? Bye, bye, cowboy.

Decision made, she felt some of the tension in her body release. The low-level buzz she felt in his presence faded away.

She didn't like how her body reacted to him (against the wishes of her brain). It was a loss of control she wasn't accustomed to.

When she reached the river, Willow stopped to let Bullet have a drink of water. They were south of the canyon, still out in the open plains. Her house sat another mile or so upriver. After standing there watching the water shimmer over the rocks for a couple minutes, she couldn't help herself. She turned around to see if she could catch one last glimpse of Zane riding off across the plains.

But he was already gone.

CHAPTER FOURTEEN

As the last sliver of sunlight disappeared, Penelope realized that she rode alone in the wilderness with no food, no map, no plan. She couldn't see the Navajo rider anymore in the velvety darkness that surrounded her, and the moon hadn't yet risen. Even if she did somehow find him, did somehow make it to the Navajo reservation, what then? Would they have any more interest in her than her mother's people?

She brought Domino to a halt, indecision gnawing at her insides like wild dogs. She could always turn around now and find her way back to Willow's house. It wasn't too late.

But, as she looked over her shoulder toward the safety of familiar territory, the howl of a lone wolf broke the night.

It was the sign she needed. The wolves had always shown

her the way in her dreams. She knew they wouldn't lead her astray now. Penelope urged Domino forward. They moved across the plains, kicking up dust and avoiding clumps of sage and cactus. When the moon rose a few minutes later, it illuminated the path before her, a single silvery strip across the land. The road leading her home. The home she'd never known.

The wolf howled again in the distance, farther away this time, and Penelope moved Domino into a trot. With the moon lighting their way, they made better progress. Time passed strangely. She knew she'd just begun, but at the same time, with a strange sense of déjà vu, it felt like this journey had been happening her whole life.

She cantered Domino here and there, onward into the great wide-open, farther than she'd ever traveled before. Everyone knew the Navajo lived this way, and the peace between them and the white people was fragile at best. She didn't know much about what had happened, only that there had been a lot of fighting, battles even, and that sometime shortly before she was born, a treaty had been signed and they'd moved to the reservation. Penelope had only seen the tribespeople a handful of times in her life. She lamented, not for the first time, how tragically little she knew of her own history.

As the hours stretched on, Penelope began to worry. What if they ran into bandits? Or stepped on a snake? Or Domino tripped in the dark or stumbled into a hole? Domino trusted her, and she would hate herself if something happened to him.

She'd had him for nearly twelve years, the truest of companions. He wasn't a young colt anymore, he approached eighteen years of age. *Please*, she thought, though to whom she directed the thought, she didn't know. *Let us get safely through this night. I just want the truth of my people.*

Another wolf howl, this time to her left, which was… south? She wasn't even sure at this point. She turned Domino off their moon path, following the sound. The moon had climbed higher now and illuminated more of the plains, a pale-yellow orb bulging just past half-full. Yearning to be whole, just as Penelope did. A shiver ran across her skin like the breath of a ghost.

And then, far in the distance, she saw lights.

Clusters of them here and there, flickering dots of orange against the black, like clouds of fireflies in the night. It could be nothing but the Navajo reservation. Wonder and trepidation spun circles in her stomach and fluttered in her chest. She couldn't believe she'd done what she'd done. Walking out on her family. Riding through the night. And now she'd actually made it.

Hoofbeats came up behind her and Penelope spun. Out of the darkness came a rider on a chestnut and white paint horse. He stopped next to her and they looked at each other. He seemed a few years older than her. Penelope knew instantly he was the lone rider she'd been following. She'd only ever seen his silhouette, but an energetic connection stretched between them that she couldn't explain.

"Hello," he said.

"Hi." She raised a hand in greeting. "I'm Penelope."

"Penelope," he repeated. "I am Atsa."

Penelope nodded. "It's nice to meet you."

Silence fell between them. Penelope didn't know what to say next. How could she explain her purpose out here in the dead of night, that she'd seen him from afar and followed him?

"Well, um, I guess I should…" she began.

Atsa raised a hand. "I know why you are here, Penelope. Follow me."

"You know?" Her mouth opened and closed a couple times.

"All will be clear soon." Atsa urged his horse forward toward the reservation.

The howl of the wolf rose into the night once again.

"Yanaha is waiting for us." He smiled over his shoulder at her.

"Yanaha?"

"My wolf."

Penelope nodded and followed him. They rode in silence toward one of the clusters of glowing lights. Penelope wondered what time it was. The moon now hung high in the sky. It had to be close to midnight, or perhaps even later.

Another hour of travel brought them to a small cluster of several buildings. Penelope stared in amazement as they rode past the first of the houses, an eight-sided log structure with earth mounded around the sides and top. Smoke spiraled up from the apex of each roof out of a small hole. Woven blankets hung in the doorways of some, where others were open, light glowing from within.

Because of the late hour, it was quiet and still. Atsa lead them past two houses and stopped in front of a dwelling that rose taller than the rest. Smoke snaked out the top of it, white against the black sky. A blanket woven in a pattern that reminded Penelope of lightning hung across the entrance. And in front of the door, waiting for them, sat a solid white wolf. It turned to them with glowing green eyes.

Atsa pointed to the beast. "The guide for your journey." He slid off his horse and patted the wolf on the head. Her tongue lolled out of the side of her mouth and she grinned toothily.

Penelope dismounted as well.

"Will your horse stay?" Atsa asked her.

Penelope nodded. She had trained Domino to ground tie a long time ago.

Atsa lifted the blanket covering the door and gestured for her to go inside. Taking a deep breath, Penelope stepped forward and ducked through the opening.

Inside, Penelope could see the artistry and skill of the symmetrical pattern of the logs. Strong and sturdy, straight sides forming the walls, then more logs that slanted upward toward the apex in the center, where the smoke escaped. More patterned rugs hung around the sides of the building, and a small bed of woven blankets lay on the far side. A table and shelf next to it were covered in an assortment of herbs, feathers, crystals, and books. And sitting in the center of the structure, on a rug next to the fire, sat a very old woman.

The woman looked up at her and smiled. "Welcome to my hogan, *shitsoi*," she said, waving a hand to indicate the house. "I am so happy you made it."

Penelope looked from the woman to Atsa and back. "*Shitsoi?* What does that mean?"

"It means grandchild," Atsa said softly.

Penelope's mouth fell open. "Grandchild?"

"Yes," the woman said. "I am Nascha. Your grandmother."

CHAPTER FIFTEEN

Felicity

The day after the thieves broke into their barn, Felicity's mother announced that they'd be having the preacher over for dinner.

"The timing couldn't be better," Felicity's mother said. "After squelching all the rumors from yesterday."

They sat in the parlor, and their housekeeper Beatrice had just brought Felicity and her mother glasses of tea. The parlor was the grandest room in the house, though the dining room gave it fair competition. Mahogany floors and walls, a marble fireplace, a grand piano in one corner which Felicity played, along with her harp, whenever they had company.

Felicity's mother paused in her knitting to take a sip of tea. "Actually," she said, lowering her voice, "It may end up being a good thing we were robbed."

"Why on earth would you say that?" Felicity asked, eyebrows raised.

"Well, to be stolen from means you have something worth stealing." Another sip of tea.

Felicity didn't think her mother would appreciate her response, so she pressed her lips into a thin line.

"Though I do hope Sheriff Longford locates our missing bridles. But about dinner tonight: we'll need to run to the butcher to get beef and prime rib and quail."

"All three?"

"Of course." Felicity's mother shot her a dark look. "We can't be too extravagant for the preacher. Don't you agree?"

"Of course, Mama," Felicity said with a nod.

"I'll need you to perform on the harp, naturally. Plus, with the fair coming up, the preacher and his wife are sure to want to see how your solo is coming along."

Felicity's insides tightened. Indeed. The song her music tutor had shamed her for a few days ago. The one which made her feel like she was plucking sinew from her own body rather than the strings of her instrument. But she just nodded again. "Yes, ma'am."

They drank their tea, Felicity's mother chattering inanely about all manner of gossip in Hawk's Hollow. Felicity found it fascinating how someone could be so terrified of being talked about in a negative light, and yet turn around and do the same to everyone else. She found her thoughts drifting to her story in her book up in the barn. Her fingers itched to take up a pen again, to be rid of her mother's irksome voice, her smothering personality, her control of every aspect of their lives…

"Felicity!" her mother shrieked.

Felicity straightened in her pink wingback chair. "Yes?"

"Were you listening to me, child?"

"Of course."

"Then why were your eyes closed?"

Felicity felt a pulse of surprise. "Were they?"

Her mother merely glared.

"I must not have slept well last night."

Her mother pursed her lips but continued. "So, what do you think?"

Felicity just nodded and said "Mmmhmm." She hadn't heard the last thing her mother had said, but it was best just to agree.

"Yes, of course you think he's a fine young man. Everyone does."

Felicity's mind raced. Her mother had to be talking about the preacher's son.

A sigh from across the room. "That would be a fine match."

The sigh, Felicity knew, was because he was white, and she was black. No matter how much money her family had, that simple fact made it out of the question. She couldn't even begin to think what kind of strings her mother had pulled to arrange this dinner. A sizeable donation to the church, no doubt.

"But I have other ideas for you," her mother continued.

"Other ideas?"

"There's a merchant in Blue Valley. He's spent his time building a very successful business but has ignored finding a good woman in his life. My contacts tell me he is now of the mind to amend that."

The way her mother said *contacts* made it sound like she had a network of spies. Felicity shivered. "How old is this man, exactly?"

"That is of no consequence," her mother said, tone shrill, eyes icy. "You are of marrying age. Beyond, really. When I was a girl, it was customary to get married when you were thirteen or fourteen. Some still do. Consider yourself very lucky."

Felicity was just shy of eighteen and couldn't imagine such a thing. "A bit antiquated, don't you think?"

"Watch your mouth with me, Felicity," her mother scolded. "We'll arrange a meeting with the Blue Valley man, Mr. Stevens, soon. After we get through with the hubbub of the annual fair. We'll be too busy with the stores until afterward."

Felicity had learned long ago to shove her feelings deep within her. No one cared about them but her, after all, and any kind of verbal or physical expression was met with harsh criticism. Numbness had become her constant companion, a cool sensation like ice spreading through her, blocking her emotions, letting nothing out. Or in.

But now, hearing her mother speak so casually of her future, as if she were some object to sell off... the lightning surged in, pulsing through her veins, arcing across her collarbones, racing up her throat to say all the things she'd been wanting to say for so many years…

She opened her mouth, cheeks tingling from the power moving through her. And that's when she noticed the glow coming off her fingers. Shock won out over the anger.

"Something to say?" her mother asked.

"No, ma'am," she said, voice trembling.

Her mother took the last sip of tea and set her glass down. "Go fetch your bonnet. We're going to the butcher."

Felicity hadn't finished her tea, but of course her mother didn't care. She got up, stiffly and disjointedly, like a puppet on strings.

"Beatrice!" her mother called.

As Felicity marched up the stairs to her room, she heard her mother giving the housekeeper lengthy instructions on cleaning the house and preparing the meal. A few minutes later, they had the wagon hitched up and they headed down the street into the commercial section of town.

When they reached the butcher shop, they tied the cart horse outside. Felicity followed her mother up the steps and through the swinging wooden doors of the store. A large glass case stood along the right side of the store. This case displayed the cuts of meat already prepared. Two tables on the back and left-hand walls were covered in carcasses waiting for the butcher's blade. Chickens, ducks, and quail, mostly. The larger ones were out back, as was the roasting spit and smoker for cooked meat.

Her mother walked gracefully to the glass counter and began to examine the cuts of meat. Felicity stood dutifully beside her, the numbness spreading over her again. She could see the other customers across the small room in the reflection off the glass, or at least a hazy version of them. So, she saw Mrs. Parker lean in close to Mrs. Wilson before she even heard their whispered-but-intentionally-not-so-quiet conversation.

"I hear vagrants broke into their barn last night," said Mrs. Parker. Her gloved hand cupped the side of Mrs. Wilson's ear as if telling some huge secret, but she cast a foxy smile over to Felicity and her mother. "I can only imagine the most desperate of souls would steal from the colored folk."

Beside her, Felicity felt her mother stiffen.

"Oh, indeed," Mrs. Wilson said with a snicker. "Poor, pathetic souls for sure. I can't imagine anything that they could possibly want."

The rage that Felicity had barely reined in at the house came back double. No, not double, a thousand-fold. She burned from the inside-out. No matter what they did, no matter that they were the wealthiest family in town, it would never amount to anything. And the most maddening part about it was that every single soul-crushing thing her mother forced down her throat was for the wholly pointless and impossible notion that it would.

She knew without looking that her hands were glowing. She

couldn't contain it, or the heat within her. The glow pulsed out from her, across the whole room. Her mother shrieked, and Felicity realized in horror that she'd seen. They'd all seen. Whatever strange magic possessed her, she'd just displayed it for them all.

But her mother wasn't pointing at her. She was pointing at the case of meat. Felicity's gaze drifted down, and she recoiled. Every piece of meat in the case had turned green, and maggots crawled in and out of them. Across the room, similar cries of dismay from Mrs. Parker and Wilson indicated they'd seen the same.

Felicity felt the heat and the rage leave her, and she began to shake. What had just happened? She looked down at her hands. The glow had dissipated, but she knew, somehow, that it had caused the meat to spoil. Before, she'd thought that maybe she was just hallucinating. But now, here, her mother and the other women saw what she'd done to the meat. It wasn't all in her head.

Which meant there was something deeply, terribly wrong with her.

CHAPTER SIXTEEN

Dynah

By the time Dynah and the doctor got back to her house, she was on the verge of hysterics. The entire ride to their homestead, the shifting black aura had clung to the doctor like a second skin. She was clearly having a mental breakdown. There could be no other explanation that made any sense at all.

Shakily, she dismounted. The doctor handed her the reins of his horse and went inside with his big black medical bag. It took everything in her power not to flinch away when his hand came close to hers. She led the horses to the stable and tied them to one of the rails. She took her time bringing them a bucket of water, from which they both drank thirstily, then untacked Moon. He was still sweaty from their strenuous gallop earlier, so she sponged him off before placing him in the corral.

Finally, she had no further excuses to keep from going inside. With dread forming a knot in her stomach, Dynah walked slowly back toward the house. A soft wind blew down through the surrounding trees, throwing dappled shadows across the ground, which only made her jumpier. What would she hallucinate next?

When she stepped inside, it was quiet. Too quiet. She fought the urge to run back to her parents' room, suddenly overwhelmed with the bizarre fear that the doctor had harmed them. But when her brisk footsteps took her to the doorway, she saw that the doctor had his stethoscope on her father's chest, her mother sitting across from him, hands clenched in prayer.

And still, the black shadow flickered around the doctor. Dynah shivered.

"How is he?" she whispered, so quietly it barely carried across the room.

Neither of them answered her. Dynah's father didn't seem conscious at all. His brow shone with sweat, and his lungs made a wet rattling sound with each labored inhale and exhale. On the bedside table next to him sat a bottle of medicine and a spoon, which it looked like the doctor had already administered.

After another minute of listening to his lungs, the doctor rose, a grim look on his face. "Pneumonia, from the looks of it."

Dynah's mother nodded, her cheeks shiny with tears.

"Keep mopping his forehead as you've been doing," he said.

"Make him drink water when he wakes up. Medicine every four hours. And keep praying."

Another nod. The doctor packed up his bag and they showed him to the door. Dynah walked back to the barn to get his horse while he continued speaking with her mother.

"I'll be back tonight, but need to check on another patient first," the doctor said as he mounted up.

When he rode off, her mother let out a sob and buried her face in Dynah's shoulder. Dynah patted her back, making comforting sounds. Surely her father was under the best care in the doctor's presence, but she couldn't help but feel immense relief that he'd gone.

"Last night there were four of us," her mother said, her voice hitching as she cried. "And now it's just you and me."

Her mother didn't mention Penelope specifically, but Dynah knew she worried about her, too. Everything had happened so suddenly. One moment Rodeo Queen had been within her grasp, now everything had gone up in smoke. It wasn't fair, not one bit. And she hated herself for even thinking that at a time like this.

"We'd better get back inside," she said softly to her mother.

She received a weary nod in response.

When they reached her father again, Dynah's mother sat down and reached into the bucket next to the bed to get fresh water. She began to dab his bright red skin.

"The water is too warm now," she said, raising her gaze up

to Dynah. "Can you go fetch a pail of fresh water from the creek?"

"Of course, Mama."

Dynah went to the kitchen to get a clean pail, then strode out the front door. She headed west into the birch forest. Not far from their house a small cascade came down from the mountains, fast and icy-cold. Before long, she could hear the rush of it through the trees. Their neighbor to the north used it, too, as it cut through the land in between the two homesteads. They had a much larger property, a ranch, really. Dynah would have a big ranch like that someday, when she married Billy or some other handsome man from Denver or Grand Junction or Tucson. She dove into her daydream as she walked to distract herself from her current predicament.

When she reached the creek, she stepped carefully across the rocks lining the bank. It was the sort of place where you could turn your ankle quite easily. Lots of little crevices and loose stone to catch your boot. At the edge, Dynah carefully leaned over and scooped up a bucketful of clear, freezing water.

She felt it the moment she straightened.

A pull in her gut, like a divining rod, so sharp it almost made her cry out. Dynah doubled over, clutching her stomach with her free hand. The tug came from across the creek. The strength of it took her breath away, and the second tug made her drop the bucket, releasing an icy torrent over her boots. She dropped to her knees, the jagged rocks bashing into her. With every passing moment, the pain intensified.

On instinct, Dynah leaned forward toward the water, toward the pull. It immediately lessened. Only minutely, but enough so that the message was clear. She had no choice but to follow it.

She left her bucket and began to make her way, with utmost caution, across the flowing water. The creek was shallow, but the current strong. Beneath the surface, algae covered the rocks, slick and slimy and treacherous. Her boots were drenched in moments, and her jeans, too, up to the knee. Slowly, slowly she made her way across the creek. When she stepped out on the other side, her gut commanded her to go right.

She entered the forest on the other side and began to jog. Whatever called to her, if she could just find it, maybe this feeling would go away. Dynah knew now, without a shadow of a doubt, that she was going mad. But she couldn't *not* follow this feeling. The pain told her that much.

The trees stopped abruptly, and Dynah found herself in a small clearing. Within the clearing, several small stone crosses rose from the grass. A shiver moved over her skin.

A graveyard.

Five tombstones, which must have belonged to the family who owned the ranch. Engravings covered each, names along with the year of birth and death. Moss crept up the base of each cross, green in some places, black in others. Somewhere off in the trees, a bird shrieked and Dynah jumped. The pain in her gut ceased as she stared down at the resting place of the five ranchers.

Another sensation took its place.

Something within her stretched out across the graveyard. A feeling like exhaling, an expansion. As that something within her reached out, searching, seeking, she felt them. The bodies within the earth. Bones, dry and brittle. And as her presence fell upon them, they shivered in their graves, answering her call.

Dynah's vision went black and her knees buckled. She staggered to the left, spun, and fainted where she stood.

CHAPTER SEVENTEEN

Willow

Practice began with the rise of the sun. Willow planned to ride all day from dawn until dusk, to mimic one day of the hundred-mile race. Also, being alone in the wilderness all day decreased her chances of running into any townsfolk. And most importantly, it kept her away from Zane.

She started out heading north along the river from her house, through the red rock canyons. Then she took Harper's Pass to cut through into the valley just north of Hawk's Hollow. From there, she alternated between a trot and a slow gallop, heading towards the Hickory Mountains.

At about nine, she made it to the foothills of the mountains. The sun climbed the sky above her, inching its way toward the heavens, but blazing hotter than hell. Sweat began to trickle down her back, and Willow adjusted her hat. She had to admit her shorn hair helped her neck stay cooler.

Her stomach brought them to a stop two hours later. She'd packed a couple tomato sandwiches, and she got one out of her saddlebag and urged Bullet forward again as she ate it. After she finished, they stopped at a creek to get a drink and splash with a little water. Bullet thought that getting Willow soaked made for a great game, and as hot as it was, Willow didn't really mind all that much.

By Willow's reckoning, they'd gone about twenty miles. When she got back on, they headed north for another hour, then cut down through a narrow canyon between Rattler Peak and White-Eyed Mountain. The rock here was gray rather than red, and it seemed to Willow less welcoming. A scuffle of falling rock brought her attention to several bighorn sheep climbing up the far side of the canyon wall. She kept her eye out for mountain lions as well. You never knew when one might try to leap down on you from a tree or overhang of rock. She'd once seen a horse hours after surviving such an attack, and it made her shiver every time she thought of it.

As Willow made her way down the canyon, she heard more falling rocks behind her, and turned to look back. She didn't see anything this time. A couple minutes later, however, she caught the sound of voices echoing off the rock walls. Voices and hoofbeats. She picked up a trot. She wasn't in the mood to chit-chat with a bunch of cowboys or traveling merchants. It would slow down her practice run. In another mile, she knew there'd be an opening in the canyon where she could head back south, which had been her planned route anyhow.

Soon, however, she heard shouts and hoofbeats ahead of her, too. Willow let out a groan. She'd picked this route because of its infrequent traffic, but apparently, luck was not with her today. Bullet swiveled her ears back, attentive to her mistress. Plus, she too could no doubt hear the riders approaching from both sides now.

Willow rounded a bend in the canyon and came upon the first group of travelers quite abruptly. Her heart dropped when she saw them. A dozen men and women, rough-looking bunch. Dirty clothes and bodies that hadn't been bathed in who knows how long. The glint of their eyes and the set of their jaws meant trouble. Willow thought the chances of them being law-abiding citizens were low. One of them could even be her father for all she knew.

She touched her hat in greeting and attempted to skirt around them, but it wasn't to be.

"Ef it it'nt the pretty boy from the town yonder," one of the men hooted.

Willow turned, and her heart sunk lower as she recognized one of the cowboys from the brawl outside the gun shop.

"How a real cowboy stay so clean, I ain't know!" said another, and this brought a whole chorus of raucous laughter.

They formed a barrier around her, blocking the narrow path forward.

"Let me pass," Willow said in her most commanding voice, low and cold. She'd learned it from her mother, and it was a voice that most obeyed. A voice that held a promise.

"I dun't think we will," said one of the men, squinting at her and spitting a wad of chewing tobacco onto the sandy canyon floor. "*Willow.*"

Willow's heart utterly stopped this time. How did they know her name? Her *real* name?

Hoofbeats sounded behind them, and Willow felt a swell of relief, though she made sure not to visibly exhale. She turned her head slightly to see how many riders there were, while still keeping an eye on the first group. A dozen riders came into view, but as they approached, they called friendly greetings to the other group. Hoots and whistles passed back and forth.

Damn it. She wasn't going to get aid from the newcomers. Things weren't looking rosy at all. Willow calculated her odds. She'd brought two guns with her today on the long ride. Two guns, twelve bullets total. She would have been hard-pressed to take down the first dirty dozen, even with an aim like hers, but two dozen? Not a chance.

But there wasn't much to be done for it. Willow placed a hand on the Colt in its holster at her right hip. "I'm not asking you again," she called to the men in front of her.

She was met, not unexpectedly, with another wave of laughter.

A swell of power rolled within her, that lightning that had

touched her during the cyclone, that heat that had visited her at the gun shop. Willow whipped both Colts out, pointed one gun in each direction, arms stretched wide, and fired from each. A wave of energy surged out of her, spreading out across the men, following the trajectory of her shots. Beneath her, Bullet shimmied in place and snorted.

Both groups of men began to shoot. But not at her. At each other.

Willow hastily backed Bullet up against the canyon wall, watching the hail of gunfire. Getting caught in the crossfire could be just as deadly, and the two groups were blocking her escape on either side. As she watched them, something even stranger happened. She saw flashes of yellow eyes, of wings, of clawed hands. Willow blinked and shook her head. The sun was clearly messing with her vision. She blinked a second time, and when she looked again, they looked like ordinary people.

She needed to get out of here, or she and Bullet were going to die.

The lightning flashed through her once again, and her voice boomed out across the canyon. "Dismount!"

The men paused in their shooting long enough to get off their horses.

"Get out of my way!" she commanded.

And they did. A part of her felt surprise, but another part, the core of lightning within her, expected nothing but complete obedience.

Willow whistled, and all their horses followed her and Bullet as she picked up a lope and moved down the canyon. When she'd gone a safe distance, she felt the flow of whatever had come over her dissipate. And then she began to shake.

What exactly had just happened?

Looking back, she saw that half the group lay injured on the canyon floor. Those remaining upright just kept on shooting, a writhing mass of chaos and destruction. How had they known who she was, and that she was a woman? She shuddered to think what would have happened had... *whatever* that was not taken charge. Maybe she could have shot her way out of there. Maybe.

Well, today clearly wasn't her day to die. Twice now this power had saved her. Strange, inexplicable, and... intoxicating. She could control people with a mere command. What else could she do? Willow felt a surge within her, an acceptance of this new challenge.

With one final look behind her, Willow urged Bullet into a trot and they left the bloody battle behind them.

CHAPTER EIGHTEEN

Penelope

Grandmother?" The word sounded foreign to Penelope. "You're *my* grandmother?"

The old woman smiled, her weathered skin crinkling around her eyes. She wore a deerskin dress, and several silver and turquoise necklaces. "Yes. You can call me your *nálí.*"

Penelope wasn't sure how to take all of this. Atsa walked past her into the house and sat down on another rug near the fire. Penelope remained frozen by the door, not sure what to do.

"Please, sit with me," Nascha said, patting the spot on the rug next to her.

Penelope crossed the room, curiosity and apprehension warring inside her. She took a seat next to Nascha. Her *nálí.* Her grandmother.

"What do you call yourself, *shitsoí?*"

"Penelope."

Nascha nodded. "I suppose you have many questions."

Now it was Penelope's turn to nod. Nascha gestured for her to ask them.

Penelope's mind spun like a compass. So many questions. It was hard to decide what to ask first. "How did you find me?"

"I never lost you, *shitsoi*," Nascha said. "But until you became a woman, it was not the right time to seek you out."

"You mean, you've known I was in Hawk's Hollow this whole time?"

"I did."

Penelope wasn't sure how to feel. She felt both anger and… happiness. That someone had been keeping track of her. Someone cared about *her*.

Nascha continued. "After your *zhé'é*—your father—died, your mother couldn't stand to be anywhere near the *Diné*."

"*Diné?*"

"The Navajo people." Nascha sighed. "It was too painful for her. She took you, and she started a new life, so she could forget. I respected that decision. While you were a girl."

Penelope thought back to her eighteenth birthday, two weeks prior. She and Willow had held a joint party since they were just a few days apart.

"But now that you are a woman, it is time for you to make your own choices." Nascha raised her arms into the air to indicate their surroundings. "And so you did. You are here."

Penelope turned to look at Atsa, who had been quiet this whole time. "It was you that I saw from the top of the buttes a few nights ago, wasn't it?"

Atsa nodded.

Penelope wanted to ask how he'd found her there, in the middle of the night. She'd woken from one of her dreams of wolves, and then she'd seen him, his horse, and his wolf. How had he known she'd be awake, and in that exact location? She didn't have the courage to ask. Not yet.

"I thought that you might be curious about the other half of your blood," Nascha said. "It called to you. And now we are together." She shrugged, as if it were completely logical, as if that explained everything.

Penelope still had so many questions. "How did my parents meet?"

Nascha pursed her lips, and Penelope thought she might be wondering why Penelope's mother hadn't told her this. But she didn't voice her thoughts, if so. "They worked on the same ranch when they were quite young, younger than you are now. Friends for several years, and then, more than that."

Penelope knew that her mother's parents had both died when she was young, so they hadn't been around to protest. She would like to think that they would have been open-minded, but so few people were.

"And… how did he—" She dropped off, unable to finish.

"How did he die?" Nascha asked gently. Her eyes went

distant as she spoke of it. "There was a dispute over some horses. One of the neighboring ranchers said that your father stole horses from him. Of course, he did not. That was proven later. But not before your *zhé'é* was shot in an argument over it."

It had been nearly twenty years, but the pain in Nascha's eyes still burned brightly. She shook her head and took a deep breath, let it back out.

"I'm sorry," Penelope said, reaching out and resting a hand on the old woman's shoulder.

Nascha straightened. "It is not for you to apologize. You must never apologize for things you are not responsible for."

Penelope opened her mouth to apologize again, then her cheeks grew hot and she nodded. After a few moments of silence, she said, "What next?"

"That is up to you, *shitsoi*. Did you only seek answers to questions, or do you wish to learn more about your people?"

Penelope realized she hadn't thought that far ahead. Everything had been a blur of impulse and gut instinct. She couldn't believe it was still the same night that she had left her home in Hawk's Hollow. Left her mother and her sister. It seemed an eternity ago.

"I think…I want to learn more. If you'll allow me."

Nascha frowned. "It is your right, *shitsoi*. You are one of us. It is not for us to allow or not allow. It is for you to claim or not claim."

Penelope nodded.

"Tomorrow we will introduce you to the rest of the clan. Your father's clan is called the Gray Streaked Dawn Clan," Nascha said. "After that, you can decide if you wish to live here, or travel between your old home and your new home."

Penelope felt a strange feeling in her chest. *New home.* Nascha had welcomed her into the clan without a moment's hesitation. In the course of a quarter-hour, she felt more seen and wanted than in her entire life in Hawk's Hollow. Tears stung the corners of her eyes.

"I'm so glad you've come," Nascha said. "You must be tired from your journey. Let us eat, and then you can rest."

Atsa got up and gathered three painted clay bowls from shelves at the back of the hogan. He returned to the fire, and Nascha ladled stew from a small iron pot into the dishes, then placed a blue biscuit into each.

"Mutton stew," Nascha explained when Penelope eyed it curiously. "And bread from blue cornmeal with juniper ash."

They sat around the fire and ate, Nascha occasionally looking up and smiling at Penelope. It felt utterly surreal to be sitting there, and yet something within her recognized it as home. The fire flickered in her eyes, and in Atsa's eyes across from her. Her mouth watered as she ate the stew and the delicious bread. She realized she'd never finished her dinner the night before. It had been quite some time since she ate, and a long journey through the plains. The longest journey of her life, in more ways than one.

When they finished their food, weariness enveloped Penelope. A full stomach, the warmth of the fire; sleep called to her. Atsa went with her as they checked on the horses one last time and brought them a bucket of water, and when they went back inside, she saw Nascha had made another bed of woven blankets on the ground a few feet away from her own. Atsa bid them goodnight and left to go back to his own hogan. Penelope laid down on her bed of blankets, her eyes heavy. She watched the flames dance, smelled the sage smoke, sweet and thick.

"Goodnight, *shitsoi*," Nascha said softly.

Sleep swirled in around her almost instantly. As did the dreams. And for once, Penelope didn't dream of wolves.

She dreamt of the night sky. Stars burned like chunks of quartz crystal. She could hear someone singing, but couldn't make out the words. Then, one by one, the stars started to go out, like candles snuffed. The darkness grew, and though Penelope had never been afraid of the dark, fear choked her now, made her sob in her sleep.

Just as the darkness became absolute, when only a handful of stars remained in the sky, there came a light. Bright and blinding and pure white. It seemed to be a comet, coming across the depths of the black night toward her, but when it drew closer, she realized the blaze of light was a horse. A horse more brilliant than fresh snow, purer than cotton blossoms in the spring.

It slowed to a trot as it came near, then stopped before her, huge and radiant. And it called her name, a mind to mind connection. The name it called was not Penelope.

"*Haséyá. Rise.*"

Penelope awoke, her heart a war hammer in her chest. Nascha was sitting up, too, watching her. The gray light of dawn blinked through the hole in the top of the hogan.

"What did you see, child?" Nascha asked.

Penelope was too shaken to answer, so she shook her head.

"You saw the darkness, didn't you?" Nascha took a deep breath, let it out. "I have seen it, too. Have felt it coming. I fear this darkness will spread over the land."

Penelope nodded, rubbing her hands over her arms to calm the goosebumps that had risen over her skin.

Nascha hooked Penelope in her gaze. "My dreams told me it was coming. As they told me you were coming. You are a part of the battle ahead."

"Me?"

"Yes. You have been brushed by the darkness. I know this from my visions, and I felt it the moment you entered this place."

"What do you mean?" Penelope shivered. "Brushed by darkness?"

"I do not know how it happened, *shitsoi.*" Nascha sighed. "But you are a part of what's to come. You will make a choice that will determine the fate of us all."

CHAPTER NINETEEN

Felicity

Felicity watched the tea kettle scream and she envied it. To be able to lose control, to let it all out… such a simple thing. Such an impossible thing. No, she was the boiling heat and the raw strength, but with no outlet.

"Beatrice!" her mother shrieked. "Take that kettle off the stove! The preacher will be here any moment!"

Felicity hastily leaned forward and lifted the kettle off the stove. The kettle ceased its banshee call with a hiss that sounded profoundly disappointed.

"Miss, do you need help?" Beatrice asked, coming up behind her.

"No, thank you," Felicity said. "Just making a bit of tea before dinner."

It was hardly an appropriate time for tea, but she'd been a

mess of anxiety since the incident at the butcher shop, and sorely in need of something to soothe her nerves. She poured the water over a cup of loose mint leaves and leaned in over the aromatic steam that wafted up.

If she could only have another three minutes alone…

Her mother bustled into the kitchen and let out another shriek. "Felicity! This is no time for tea!"

"I have a stomachache," Felicity said. Which was true. A stomachache caused by anxiety.

"Well, you'll just have to grin and bear it. Our guests will be here any moment!"

"Beatrice. *Please.*" Her mother glared at the housekeeper. No one else could say *please* in quite so demanding a fashion.

Beatrice stepped forward, face carefully neutral, and gently took the teacup from Felicity's grasp. Felicity relinquished without argument, though a sigh escaped her lips.

"Pull it together," her mother snapped, and strode out into the hall. "Come along," she called over her shoulder.

They adjourned to the parlor, where Felicity's father waited, smoking a pipe and reading a magazine.

"Harold, honestly!" Felicity's mother said, waving a hand in the air and coughing with great exaggeration.

Felicity had to stifle a giggle. Her father rolled his eyes with great aplomb and went to put his pipe in his study. The doorbell rang. Felicity's mother looked like she might explode, from several different emotions at once. They took their seats in the parlor, sitting primly on the elegant furniture. Felicity's father came back last, and as soon as he sat down, Beatrice opened the front door to greet their dinner guests.

"Preacher, how lovely to see you!" Felicity's mother said, moving across the room in a sweep of petticoats. "And Abigail!"

The preacher and his wife spoke similar greetings, then the preacher said, "You remember our son, Travis."

"Of course!"

Felicity wondered if her mother realized how fake she sounded, how strange her smile looked stretched so widely across her face.

They began in the parlor, Beatrice pouring everyone drinks: brandy for the men, lemonade for everyone else. Conversation started light: the weather, the upcoming fair, school for Felicity and Travis. Felicity caught Travis shooting her furtive glances from beneath his blonde lashes. They knew each other from school and church but had barely spoken a word to each other. Of course, almost no one spoke to Felicity.

Next, they retreated to the dining room, where Beatrice served the braised beef, prime rib, stuffed quail, greens, potatoes, and bread. Felicity couldn't touch the meat, not after what she'd seen earlier. Her mother, however, had no such compunction. Dessert was bread pudding with peach glaze. Felicity's mother gave Beatrice glowing compliments that never left her mouth except in front of guests.

After dinner, it was back to the parlor for Felicity to entertain the guests. She started on the harp, playing Mozart and Handel. Beatrice served coffee in little white china cups. Next, Felicity moved to the piano. She played a couple of songs, and then, to her immense surprise, Travis stood and said, "Would you mind if we played a duet?"

Felicity looked to her mother, whose shock registered for the barest of moments before another face-splitting smile moved across it. The other adults offered hearty encouragement. Travis approached the grand piano, and Felicity slid over to allow him space on the bench.

As he took his seat, Felicity realized this was the closest she'd sat to a boy in her whole life. Her mother had made sure of that. She could feel the warmth from Travis's body. He cast her a smile which seemed genuine.

"Do you know Beethoven's Moonlight Sonata?" he asked softly.

"Of course," she responded, then blushed at her somewhat rude retort.

Travis just grinned and raised his hands above the keys. "Ready?"

She nodded.

"Three, two, one…"

The song began in perfect harmony. Felicity had only ever played duets with her father, and that had been years ago. It was actually…pleasant. Unlike her harp playing. Travis looked over at her and smiled as he played, and she found herself smiling back. They didn't miss a beat, staying in perfect sync for the entirety of the song. When they finished, the room filled with applause, including Beatrice, who stood in the corner.

"Bravo!" said the preacher. "That was wonderful."

"You are splendid on both the piano and the harp," Abigail said.

"You are," Travis added.

Felicity's cheeks flamed. "You are very talented, too," she said shyly.

"I have a marvelous idea!" Abigail said. She turned to look expectantly at her husband.

"Oh—oh, yes! Perfect!" he exclaimed.

Felicity and her parents exchanged glances.

"We've been discussing how to take the musical performance at the fair up a notch," the preacher said. "And I think we have our answer." He pointed both hands at Felicity and Travis. "I know you're already playing the harp, Felicity, but adding the piano duet would be spectacular."

Abigail smiled. "As long as your parents give permission."

"Of course," Felicity's mother said, that same too-big smile pasted on her face. "We're so flattered."

"You're going to bring a piano down to the arena?" Felicity's father asked. He grinned. "Now that's something I'd like to see."

"We'll just have to make it work," the preacher said.

"We have another week to figure out the details," Abigail

said.

Felicity and Travis returned to their chairs, and the two families conversed for another half-hour. After that, Abigail pronounced it time for them to be getting home. Everyone said their farewells and Beatrice held the door for their guests. They watched and waved from the door as they loaded up in their wagon and rolled away from the house.

As soon as the door was shut, Felicity's mother dragged her aside, her fingers crushing in their strength. "What was that boy whispering to you by the piano?"

Felicity gasped from the pain of her mother's grip. "He was asking what songs I knew!"

"That was all, was it?"

Felicity pulled her arm away, her eyes stinging with tears.

"If he thinks you're one of those *loose* girls, just because we weren't brought up like everyone else around here..." her mother hissed, venomous as a snake.

"Mama, no—"

"I am *not* going to have your marriage to the Blue Valley merchant ruined...*spoiled*...by any foolishness."

The indignity of it all was too much. She'd received genuine praise and excitement about her musical talent for the first time in her life, shared a smile with a boy, the *preacher's* son, and her mother thought her virtue was at stake?

The words came out with the force of a geyser. She was miles beyond tea kettle. "Did it ever occur to you that I don't want you to choose a husband for me? That maybe, I don't want a husband at all?"

Her mother's eyes widened with shock. She grabbed Felicity's arm again, pushed her against the wall. "It doesn't matter what you want, ungrateful girl!" She slapped her cheek, not hard enough to leave a mark, but hard enough to sting like hell. "You will do what we tell you! And I will be accompanying you to every practice. You will not so much as *breathe* without my permission, do you understand?"

Felicity did understand. And the lightning within her did, too. It acted of its own accord, pulsing off Felicity's body and into her mother, forcing her back.

Her mother went still, unsure of what had just happened. She raised a hand, and Felicity felt sure another slap was in order. The next moment her mother doubled over, clutching her stomach, and ran for the bathroom, where she proceeded to retch up her entire dinner.

Felicity stood, heart pounding, listening for several long moments. The lightning slowly faded away, the glow leaving her fingertips. She knew she should go check on her mother. But instead, she turned and walked out to the barn to fetch her book.

CHAPTER TWENTY

Dynah

When Dynah came to in the graveyard, she panicked so severely she nearly fainted again. But this time, the skeletons beneath the earth did not speak to her. *Call* to her. She got up off the ground and ran back to the creek.

By the time she got back to the cabin with a fresh bucket of water, her mother was in a tizzy.

"Where have you *been*?"

Dynah glanced up at the clock on the wall. It had only taken her an extra twenty minutes or so. "Sorry, Mama, I twisted my ankle by the creek and had to rest for a bit before I could walk on it again."

Her mother grabbed the bucket of cold water and returned to the bedroom. "Don't come in here. I don't want you catching it, too."

Dynah waited in her bedroom. Time stretched on torturously. Worrying about her father. Worrying about Penelope. Trying to find a way to justify what had happened to her at the graveyard.

She would have to confess to her mother that she'd gone quite insane. And then she'd be sent to that mental hospital in Long Pines where people went and never came back. Normal hospitals seemed to have the goal of treating patients and then releasing them back into the world. But not those with problems in their heads. No, those were simply designed to keep people in, away from ordinary folk.

Ordinary folk.

Dynah choked back a sob. She couldn't burden her mother with this right now. After her father was better—if he got better—then she'd tell her. And maybe, just maybe, if stress had brought this on it would go away eventually. Then she wouldn't have to tell anyone the things she'd seen. The things she'd *felt*.

The minutes passed by like honey, slow and sticky. It was so quiet she could hear the ticking of the clock, hear the soft murmur of her mother in the next room praying. As the day wore on, Dynah moved out into the sitting room. Around four, she made dinner for herself and her mother; roasted chicken with beans and corn.

Twice she had to make runs for more cold water. Too scared to return to the creek by the graveyard, she rode Moon bareback to another much farther away. Her mother was too preoccupied to notice.

As afternoon faded into evening, the doctor came back to check on them. Dynah watched him and his black aura with a growing sense of dread. It seemed even bigger and darker than it had this morning. He declared her father's condition worse and not better, and helped her mother give him more medicine. They whispered together at the bedside, and at one point the doctor reached out and rested a hand on her mother's hand. Her mother's face crumpled. It could mean only one thing.

Night fell, full and heavy and bleak. The doctor had left hours ago. Or had it been minutes? Dynah couldn't tell any longer. She stared out the window, counting the stars as they came out, watching the moon climb higher and higher. She wished her mother would let her help attend to her father. Anything but sitting here, waiting for him to die.

And where the hell was Penelope? How could she abandon them at a time like this? Not that her sister had known Roy would fall so ill. But it still seemed unfair, that she should be off galivanting around when Dynah and her mother were stuck here in this cycle of misery.

Worry for Penelope tempered her anger. Her sister was probably at Willow's house—and if so, Dynah wanted to curse her out. But if she wasn't…what if something had befallen her, a woman alone out in the world?

Around midnight, Dynah made up her mind.

She told her mother she was going to bed, which her mother barely acknowledged. Then she waited fifteen minutes in the dark of her room before she opened the window and crawled out. A thrill ran through her as she did—she'd never snuck out before. Penelope did all the time, but Dynah had watched her before and she only ever went out into the forest. Dynah seriously doubted she was meeting boys or getting into any mischief. But still, it wasn't *allowed*, and so Dynah had never done it herself. Until now.

Amongst the shadows and the songs of the crickets, she tiptoed out to the barn. Moon snorted and nickered as she approached, not seeming at all concerned by her nighttime visit. He seemed to glow in the darkness, a sterling glimmer of stars. Dynah's emotions came surging out of her, and she pressed her face into his soft shoulder and let the tears she'd been holding the last twenty-four hours escape.

Around Moon, she could be totally herself. He was the only one who didn't care what she looked like. Didn't judge her, expect things of her. Lust after her or envy her. He was just a horse, and she was just a girl.

When she'd spent all her tears, she slipped on his bridle and mounted bareback again. Then she headed for Willow's house. It sat on the complete opposite side of Hawk's Hollow. Whereas Dynah's house was directly west of town, only three miles out, Willow's was much farther south and much farther east. She'd only been there once, but she reckoned she had about eight miles ahead of her. In the dead of night.

She headed south first to skirt about the town, making sure not to get too close in case anyone awake spotted her. It wouldn't do any good at all to get caught. Once she got out of the birch forest near her house and onto open ground, she loped Moon to pass the journey more quickly. Overhead, her horse's namesake illuminated their path.

After she passed to the south of town, cutting between the railroad station and the public arena, she headed east toward the river. The land was mostly flat and clear here, and she made good time. She slowed back down to a walk when, an hour and a half later, she approached the river and the ground became rocky. Once she got within sight of the water, she headed north.

Trees began to pop up here and there, and Dynah steered Moon into a red rock canyon. Willow's house had to be close. It had been years since she'd been there, and that had been during the day. Dynah didn't recall that Willow had any neighbors in this area, at least she certainly hoped not. She didn't want to get shot for trespassing.

Finally, she saw the outline of Willow's small cabin in the distance. She let out a sigh of relief, and Moon snorted to echo the emotion. As she covered the last few hundred yards, Dynah began to wonder how she'd wake Willow up at this time of night without getting shot.

When they were a few feet away from the house, Moon tripped and Dynah barely stopped herself from falling off over his shoulder. She heard a loud clattering sound, followed by the clucking of chickens and the snort of a couple horses. A moment later, a tall, lanky boy came rushing out of the cabin, rifle in hand.

"You've got a barrel's-worth of rock salt pointed at your face," came a low, gravelly voice. "You'd better state your business *real* damn fast."

"I'm here to see Willow!" Dynah shrieked, holding her hands up. "I'm her friend Dynah!"

"Dynah?" A long pause. "I think the term *friend* is a bit of a stretch."

"Willow?" she gasped. "You—I thought you were—"

"A man?" Dynah could hear the smirk in Willow's voice. "That's the point."

"Why would you want to be a man?"

Dynah got only a sigh in response. "I wouldn't expect you to understand. Why are you at my house in the middle of the damn night?"

"What was that sound? It seemed like Moon tripped on something…"

"That would be my trip-wire."

Dynah's eyebrows shot up. "You have this place booby-trapped?"

"There have been… *strange* things going on around here. It seemed prudent." Willow sighed and lowered her gun finally. "Listen, Dynah. It's late. Why are you creeping around out here?"

"I'm not creeping. I'm looking for Penelope." Dynah tried to keep the desperation from her voice and failed.

A very long pause. "Penelope? She's gone?"

"Oh, God." Dynah felt a shudder move up her ribcage and into her throat. "If she's not here, then—" She couldn't finish.

Willow took a couple steps closer. "Tell me what happened," she said, her voice softening a tad.

"Two nights ago, she got in a huge fight with Roy. I don't know what came over her."

"Probably tired of Roy being a jerk," Willow said drily.

"Well, it wasn't like her. And anyway, he's probably about to die now!" Dynah wailed. She slumped over onto Moon's neck and cried in his mane.

"Wait, what?"

But Dynah couldn't speak for nearly a minute. When she'd finally pulled herself together, she sniffled and continued. "Penelope stormed off. And then Roy got sick. The doctor's been out and everything, but he's only getting worse."

"Uh…sorry."

Dynah could tell Willow wasn't any good at comforting people. She sniffled again.

"So, Penelope didn't say where she was going?"

Dynah shook her head. "I thought she'd come here. Where else would she go?"

"Her tribe, obviously," Willow retorted.

Dynah went stiff. "Her tribe? The Indian tribe?"

"The Navajo, yes," Willow said in a patient and only slightly condescending tone. "They're half her blood. She's been wanting to learn more about that side of herself for… well, as long as we've been friends."

It made sense, Dynah supposed. But how had she not known this about her own sister?

"So, Roy might die?" Willow asked.

Dynah could see her face in the moonlight. She was chewing her bottom lip softly as if contemplating something. "Yes, probably," she answered flatly. "That's what the doctor told my mother."

Willow sighed. "Well, I suppose I need to go find her, then. She doesn't have much love for the man, but I'm sure she wants to be there for you and your mama."

"Really?" It shocked her that Willow would embark on a journey into Navajo territory. She didn't know what to say. "I, um, well I'd go with you, but I need to help my mama."

Willow nodded. "It'll be quicker if I go alone anyway. I'll go get Bullet now."

"In the middle of the night?"

"Well, you're out here, aren't you?"

Dynah shrugged. "Okay, then." A pause. "I don't know how to thank you."

"You can owe me. I'll think of something later." Willow grinned. She looked excited to be headed out in the middle of the night.

"Well, I'll wait for you to get your mare. We might as well ride part of the way together since we're headed the same direction."

Willow nodded and headed back into her house. A few minutes later she came from around the back, mounted up on her chestnut mare, rifle at her side, a pistol at each hip. They flashed in the moonlight.

"Let's head out," she said.

The girls rode in silence at first, back along the river until they left the red rock canyon, then west across the plains. Something kept turning over in Dynah's mind, like a pebble tumbled in a stream. She wanted to ask Willow if she'd seen the lightning that day during the sandstorm. Willow had said something about strange things happening. Maybe they'd experienced the same things? But Dynah couldn't get up the nerve to ask. Willow already looked at her with disdain, and she'd only sound like a crazy person. No, she'd just have to wait until her sister got back.

If Willow could find her.

CHAPTER TWENTY-ONE

Willow

Just past the train station, Willow and Dynah parted ways. Dynah headed her gray gelding north, and Willow kept due west. The early summer heat which clung to the earth long after the sun went down had finally dissipated from the desert plains. It was that cool, quiet, purple part of the night, past the moon's zenith and inching towards dawn.

When the sun finally did begin to peek up along the horizon, Willow felt it more than she saw it, being behind her in the east. A lightening of the sky, both in color and weight. A stir in the slumber of the planet. And there was something else. Willow realized, without knowing when or how it started, that she could *feel* Penelope.

It felt kind of like firing her gun. Sighting down the length of the barrel at her target. Her finger squeezing the trigger, soft and light. The gunfire, the pop as bullet hit target. In between all of that, there existed a moment when she knew if she would make the shot or not. A line of connection between her gut and her goal.

This felt the same way.

She couldn't explain it, but then, there'd been a lot of things she couldn't explain lately. The connection between her and her best friend told her to turn south, so she did. And as a line of plum and persimmon began to flame along the horizon to her left, and the sun began its inevitable, inexorable climb, she saw a rider off in the distance.

As the rider approached, Willow stiffened. Buckskin horse. Black-haired man. Lean muscles and blue eyes. Well, she couldn't see the eyes yet. But she knew who it was.

"I'm beginning to think you're followin' me, cowboy," Zane said in his musical drawl.

A shiver, quickly suppressed. "That would be interesting, being as how I'm coming from the opposite direction."

Zane chuckled and pulled his horse to a halt, so they faced each other. "I'm just messing with you. I know what you're doing out here."

"Do you?" She raised her brows.

"Practicing. Just like I am."

"Not this time. I'm actually looking for a friend."

Zane stared at her, the edges of his lips quirked up. "At the crack of dawn? You must have departed hours ago."

Willow shrugged. "It's a matter of some urgency."

"Well, mind if I join you?"

Yes. No. Oh, hell... "If you don't mind traveling into Navajo territory."

Zane's lips quirked even further. "Are you friendly with the Navajo?"

"Well, my best friend is half Navajo, and she's on the reservation at the moment."

"She? Your best friend is a girl?"

Willow bit her lip. She hadn't meant to say that. This was *exactly* why she shouldn't be spending time with Zane. "Woman, not girl. And yes."

"Okay." Zane's gaze penetrated her, as if searching her very soul. "And no, I don't mind. I need to add some miles to my practice run anyway."

"Well, follow me, then." Willow squeezed her legs to Bullet's sides, and they continued.

Since the sun had risen and she could see, Willow moved Bullet into a lope to make better time. They moved across the plains, and Willow made a game in her head of chasing the fresh sunbeams as they stretched across the earth, the illumination moving farther and farther west. She relaxed somewhat and almost forgot about the cowboy riding at her side.

After an hour of alternating between a trot and a lope, they let the horses walk. Willow swung off and pulled down the water skin she'd hung behind her saddle. She offered water to

Bullet first, then took a sip herself, then offered some to Zane. He nodded and took a swig, and she tried not to watch as a trickle of water ran down his lips and jawline.

Dear God. Get ahold of yourself.

Zane handed back the water skin, and they remounted and continued at a walk.

They'd traveled in silence for a good while, and Willow had grown sick of it. She looked over at him. "So, you've been sort of mysterious about where you came from, but maybe you can tell me some of the places you've been?"

Zane met her gaze. "I can do that. If you tell me more about this best friend of yours."

Willow nodded. "Deal."

Zane leaned back in the saddle, one hand resting on his thigh. "I've been all over, really. Denver. Fort Worth. San Antonio. Santa Fe. Tombstone. Sheridan."

Willow tried not to look as impressed as she was. And as jealous. "Oh, yeah? And what do you typically do when you're not entering races?"

He shrugged. "A little bit of this and that. Mostly helping out on ranches. Done some work on railroads." He looked over at her. "That was two questions, you cheater. Your turn."

"My friend. Right." Willow nodded. "Her name is Penelope. We've known each other since we were babies. I mean, as long as we can remember. Three or four years old."

"That's a long time." Zane cast his eyes in Willow's direction.

"Usually after the age of seven or eight boys and girls start playing more with their own."

Willow fidgeted in her saddle. He just wasn't going to let it go, was he? "Well, I think we remained friends because neither of us have fathers. We were both outcasts. So, we stayed outcasts together."

"Oh? Your dad passed away?"

Now it was Willow's turn to shrug. "I mean, not that I'm aware of. He just didn't stick around. It's just been me and my mother as long as I can remember."

"Sorry to hear that."

"He's an outlaw. Probably for the best." It was a lie, and Willow knew it. And by the way Zane cocked his head, she figured he knew it, too.

"I'm sure Penelope had it doubly bad being half Navajo," Zane commented. "Not fitting in on either side. I know a bit what that's like."

His voice softened on the last sentence, and Willow darted a glance over at him. He held it in well, but she could see a churn of emotion in those blue eyes.

"And why must we find Penelope so urgently?" Zane asked.

Willow realized he'd accompanied her over an hour and still didn't know why she sought the reservation. "Her stepfather has fallen ill."

"Oh?" Zane cocked an eyebrow. "What's he have?"

"I don't know. It's pretty bad, though." Willow looked down

at the horn of her saddle. "It may be her last chance to say goodbye. Well, mostly to support her mother and sister. Penelope doesn't actually get along well with him."

As the words came out of her mouth, Willow wondered why her mouth had run away with her. Something about Zane just made her feel like she could tell him anything. Or maybe she was being a chatterbox because of the butterflies swooping around inside her ribcage.

"I don't get along well with my father, either," Zane said. He fell silent a moment. "Have you ever thought about trying to find yours?"

"Oh, yes," she blurted out. "That's one of the things I want to do when I leave Hawk's Hollow."

"And how does your mother feel about that?"

Willow laughed. "I'm not planning on mentioning it. I doubt she'd be keen on the idea. And she's not a woman you want mad at you."

Zane laughed. "I can imagine she's pretty tough if she fell in love with an outlaw."

"That she is."

The sun had risen high in the sky by now, and it punished them with its intense heat. It wasn't even ten in the morning, and Willow could see shimmering waves rising up from the sands beneath the horses' hooves. Other than a string of mountains, far, far, in the distance, she couldn't see a damn thing in any direction. Just wide-open emptiness. She'd never gone anywhere near this far south.

They urged the horses into a faster pace again, starting up their trot-lope intervals. After another hour, sweat drenched Bullet and Willow both. The binding around her chest chafed and chafed until it felt like a hot brand, and Willow cursed inwardly. Damn Hawk's Hollow and its antiquated ways. She shouldn't have to pretend to be a man just to enter a blasted race. There were plenty of daring ladies all over the West. Annie Oakley. Calamity Jane. Pearl Hart. Belle Star.

When a silver creek appeared across the plains in front of them, Willow wanted to kiss the sky. They rode the horses to the water's edge and dismounted. Bullet stepped into the water and shoved her nose into it, splashing Willow and Zane both. Zane laughed.

"Your horse has the right idea!"

And with that, he stripped off his boots, followed by his plaid shirt and his hat, and waded out farther into the creek. Willow's heart stuttered to a stop. She watched as Zane scooped handfuls of water onto his chest. He splashed his face and then flipped his head over and dunked the top of it. When he straightened, he shook the excess droplets out of his midnight hair. The movement made his deeply tanned skin ripple over his muscles. Every bit of him was hard, taut, tantalizing.

"Aren't you coming?" Zane called. "You've got to be dying!"

"Uh, no," Willow said. "I'm okay."

"Don't be a kidder! It's blazing out here!"

When she stayed stubbornly in the shallows, Zane waded over toward her. She eyed him warily as he approached. He stopped about five feet away, every inch of his glorious body dripping with water.

"Can I tell you a secret, Will?"

Willow nodded.

"I know you're a girl."

Willow's mouth fell open. "What?" It came out shrill as a train whistle.

"Woman—sorry!"

"No, I mean—I—how do you know?"

Zane laughed. "I'm sorry, but it's the most obvious thing in the world."

"How?" Willow sputtered. "Why?"

"Well…" Zane ran a hand through the hair at the back of his head. "You're kinda pretty, for starters."

And this, after her intense surprise, Willow just couldn't stomach. "*Kinda?*"

Zane laughed again, deep and long. "Ahh," he finally managed when his mirth had settled. "I rest my case."

"Wait a second!" Willow pointed an accusatory finger at him. "You were trying to get me to take my clothes off!"

"I knew you weren't going to." He grinned. "But seriously, though. It's hot as hell. At least soak your shirt or something. I won't look—promise."

"Fine. Go over there." Willow shoved a finger toward the

opposite bank of the creek.

Zane made a small bow and did as requested, backing away from her. When he reached the far side of the water, he turned around, facing away. "Eyes closed and everything," he called.

A gentleman cowboy. Willow supposed they came along once in a blue moon. She quickly unbuttoned her shirt and submerged it in the water, then splashed water over her face and chest. She made sure to get some on her chafe marks, which stung, but felt better after. Then she wrung out her shirt and put it back on. Finally, she took off her hat and dunked her hair as Zane had done.

"Okay. You can turn around."

He did as she said, and their eyes met. It was a different kind of look, now that she knew he knew. She didn't have to pretend to be something she wasn't. And the look in his eyes told her he had been pretending, too. Pretending not to notice her. They drank each other in like they hadn't been able to before.

"Okay then," Willow said a bit unsteadily. "We'd better get going."

Zane nodded and they remounted.

"Did you know right away?" Willow asked as they picked up a trot.

"Pretty much," he said. "I thought, *damn,* this woman can throw a mean punch."

Willow laughed.

"So, what do I call you now?" he asked.

"Willow," she said.

And she urged Bullet into a lope as they continued into the vastness before them.

CHAPTER TWENTY-TWO

Penelope

We will discuss how to face this darkness together," Nascha told Penelope. "But first, let us celebrate this day. The day you meet your clan."

Penelope nodded, and they spoke no more of the darkness as they ate a breakfast of leftover blue bread, wolf berries, and wax currants.

"So, does Atsa work for you?" Penelope asked, to start a lighter conversation.

"In a manner of speaking. He is my apprentice."

"Apprentice?" Penelope realized she didn't know what her *náli* did.

"I am one of the clan shamans," Nascha said.

Penelope's eyes widened. "Shaman? You do magic?"

Nascha laughed. "Magic, as you call it, is everywhere, girl. It speaks to everyone. But only some of us listen."

"But…how does it work? What do you use it for?"

"I listen to nature. I perform rituals for the clan. I heal illnesses in my people."

Penelope had never heard someone talk of such things. How many other things had she missed out on her whole life?

"Do not worry," Nascha said. "You will learn."

A shiver ran through Penelope. Could the woman read her thoughts?

"And the first thing you will learn, if you wish, is your Navajo name. The name we gave you when you were born."

"Yes," Penelope said. "I would very much like to know that."

"The name you were given at your birth is *Haséyá*."

"*Haséyá*," Penelope repeated, letting it roll off her tongue. Then she gasped. "I dreamed that name last night. What does it mean?"

Nascha smiled. "It means, 'she rises'."

And Penelope remembered the white horse calling her to rise, and she didn't think any name could be more perfect than this name.

Nascha told her more about the Gray Streaked Dawn Clan, and the rest of the Diné, their history and traditions and the names of relatives Penelope would meet later. An hour passed, maybe two. There was a knock on one of the logs outside the hogan, and Atsa ducked inside. "Good morning," he said.

"Good morning," Penelope echoed.

"The clan has gathered, as requested," Atsa said to Nascha.

"Thank you," Nascha said. "I am sure the others are excited to meet their long-lost sister."

Penelope knew she meant *sister* in the broader term. It sent a happy shiver through her. She had a family now. A big family.

"After you meet the rest of the clan," Nascha said, "We can discuss how long you'd like to stay."

As the minutes passed, Penelope began to feel a buzz of nervous energy in her stomach, as if she'd swallowed a whole hive of bees. The whole clan was gathering to see *her*. No one had ever paid her any attention at all, not in her whole life. Not the positive kind of attention, that is. The idea of standing before a large group of people, the center of attention, made her nauseated.

They stepped outside, and Nascha walked on ahead of them. Atsa caught her eye, seeming to sense her nervousness. "You are the granddaughter of the great shaman Nascha. The blood of the Diné flows in your veins. There is nothing to fear, *Haséyá*."

Penelope blinked, absorbing his words. Her stomach settled. She followed him past several hogans to a large log building that stood beyond the dwellings a good distance away. A crowd had already gathered, several hundred in total.

"These people can't possibly all live here—there aren't enough hogans!" Penelope gasped.

"The Diné live in many small groups spread across the land," Atsa said. "The ones who do not live here with us traveled to meet you."

All of these people had come from afar to see her? Penelope's heart raced, but she remembered Atsa's words and took a deep, steadying breath. When they reached the head of the crowd, Nascha strode to the center and addressed the clan.

"Greetings, Gray Streaked Dawn Clan. Today is a very special day. Today I have the honor to introduce you to someone who left us a long time ago. Someone very dear to me, my granddaughter *Haséyá*."

Nascha waved an arm in Penelope's direction, and Penelope, unsure what to do, raised a hand and waved at the huge crowd. They erupted in cheers and shouts, and many raised their fists into the air. Penelope smiled, and her heart felt full, fuller than it ever had before. Atsa caught her eye again and smiled back.

"Let us celebrate this beautiful day!" Nascha called.

And celebrate they did. Penelope soon realized the purpose of the larger building as she smelled the smoke wafting up from it, and people began to carry out trays of food to set out along a series of tables. Music began to play, drums and other instruments, and circles of dancers sprung up throughout the gathering.

Everyone wanted to meet their long-lost clanswoman, and so Penelope stood with Nascha and they greeted person after person. Atsa left to get them food, and Penelope realized when he handed her a steaming bowl of corn and beans that she felt famished. Her lips soon grew tired after so much smiling, but it was a good tired. A happy tired.

The festivities continued all day, until the sun set in a glorious display of flame and cactus-flower fuchsia. They continued as the stars popped out, one by one, like a sharpshooter hitting a target. They continued as the moon rose high in the sky, and the furious heat of day finally dissipated. They continued through the night, as comets streaked across the velvety black and Nascha told tales to children and adults alike.

Penelope wasn't sure what time it was, late night or early morning, when she found herself staring deliriously across a fire at Atsa. Delirious from lack of sleep and delirious from joy. Like a small child, determined to stay up until the break of dawn just for the hell of it, no matter how sleepy she got. As she sat and stared into the fire, at the strange figures that seemed to leap about within the flames, animals and birds and winged beings that were neither and both, she suddenly found herself looking beyond the light into the face of the boy who had found her.

Well, the man. If only by a little. Her guide. How *had* he found her? She still hadn't summoned the courage to ask him. For now, she was content with the mystery, because she'd just noticed how very beautiful he was. How the red of the flames made his skin glow a deeper, more vibrant color. How his long, black hair seemed to soak up the night. How his dark eyes reflected the stars.

Her whole life she'd been told that white skin equated to beauty. Not verbally, of course. But in the actions of all those around her. How Dynah, with her pale marble skin and flame-red hair, was the prettiest thing around. How her sister had gotten her looks from their mother, who looked just the same. And all the other coveted women in Hawk's Hollow, all with their skin so much lighter than Penelope's.

So, it came as a revolution inside her, Atsa's beauty, and Penelope lost herself in it for a countless span of time. Until the subject of her study suddenly sat down next to her, and Penelope wondered in horror if he had noticed her watching him.

She blurted out the question to divert his attention elsewhere. "How did you find me?"

"Find you?" He cocked his head to the side.

"That first night. When I climbed to the top of the buttes."

Atsa smiled. "What makes you think it's not the other way around? Perhaps *you* found *me*."

Penelope went still. That had never occurred to her, but she supposed it was possible. She *had* spotted him, from her place atop the canyon, and also the night before out on the plains. Her head spun as she pondered it, but only for a moment, because she was far too tired to put much thought into it.

"Perhaps," Atsa continued, "The song in your heart found its singer." He waved a hand around at the clan. At their people.

And they sat there beside each other until the first rays of dawn lightened the sky.

Tendrils of smoke from the fire still rose into the air when Penelope awoke a few hours later. Atsa yawned and stretched beside her. The sun beat down on them, directly overhead.

One of her clansmen approached. "There are two white men here to see you, *Haséyá*." He pointed toward the edge of the crowd.

Penelope sat up, confused. When she turned, she saw one familiar face and one not-so-familiar. *Willow?* "What are you doing here?" Penelope asked as they approached.

"It's bad news, I'm afraid." Willow's face was stormy. "It's Roy. He's real sick, Pen."

Penelope could feel Atsa come to stand behind her. "Roy?" he asked.

"My stepfather." Penelope chewed on her lip. She remembered her fight with Roy, and how her anger had seemed to propel *into* him. How he'd bent over, coughing, and she'd made her escape. Guilt reared up within her.

"I know you and Roy don't see eye to eye," Willow said. "But Dynah needs you."

"She said that?" Penelope's eyebrows raised to the sky.

Willow nodded. "She rode to my house in the middle of the night. She couldn't come here herself since she's helping your mother take care of him."

Penelope felt a thunderstorm of emotions wash through her. Guilt mixed with anger mixed with pity mixed with surprise, and a good portion of satisfaction thrown in for good measure. Roy had always been awful to her. It was no worse than he deserved. And now Dynah suddenly wanted her sister? Irony was a cruel master. She had finally found a family who wanted her, who *saw* her, and now the family that had always looked down its nose on her needed her to come back.

But family was family.

"I need to find my *náli*," Penelope said.

"Your what?" Willow asked.

"Grandmother," she said.

"She's over there," Atsa said, pointing toward the large communal building.

Penelope found Nascha and explained the situation.

Nascha's lips pressed into a grim line, but she nodded. "I understand, *shitsoi*. But we must discuss further the dream you had. Soon."

"I'll be back," Penelope said firmly.

"I know you will," Nascha said, pulling her into a hug. "I'll send some cedar bark and sage to help your mother's husband in his healing process."

They walked back to Nascha's hogan. The shaman went inside and came back a couple minutes later with several leather pouches.

"Thank you, *nálí*," Penelope said. Her eyes welled with tears, and she could feel her heart breaking. She wasn't ready to leave. She'd only just reunited with everyone.

"I will escort you to the edge of Diné territory," Atsa said.

They gathered the horses and he led the way, beyond the hogans and into the plains for several miles. The late afternoon heat settled over the earth like a bed of burning coals. Lizards sunned on rocks and buzzards circled overhead, looking for their next meal.

At some unseen border, Atsa stopped and bid them farewell. "Good luck, *Haséyá*. I hope we see you again soon."

"You will," Penelope said with a firm nod.

The ride back to Penelope's house (or was it her old house?) took the remainder of the day. Zane, who Penelope had come to learn was Willow's new friend, departed shortly before they arrived. As shadows began to devour the last of the sun's rays, they reached the home she had grown up in. It seemed an eternity had passed, though it had only been two days.

Dynah came running outside before they even reached the front door. "Penelope!"

For a moment, Penelope thought her sister would hug her, but she stopped a couple feet away and they stared at each other awkwardly. "So, Roy?" Penelope finally said.

"I need to head home and check on the chickens," Willow said, making her escape. Penelope knew her friend had no interest in caring for the ill.

"Thank you," Dynah said to Willow. "Really."

"Don't worry about it." Willow moved Bullet into a trot and headed south.

"How's mother?" Penelope asked as they took Domino to the barn.

"Not good." Dynah's brow wrinkled and her face went red and splotchy. "I—I don't think father—Roy—will make it—" and Dynah cut off, her voice choked with tears.

"I brought some herbs from my clan," Penelope said, patting the leather pouches tied to her saddlebag.

"What will those do?" Dynah asked suspiciously.

"Help him heal," Penelope said in a tone that brokered no argument. If they wanted her help so desperately, they would have to accept what she offered. She was not the same Penelope who had left forty-eight hours ago. Silence and acquiescence were her false gods no longer.

She strode into the house, Dynah at her heels, and made her way back to the bedroom. Her mother looked up weakly, hopelessly, as Penelope entered the room. Their eyes met, and an understanding passed between them. Though they had never been close, they were still mother and daughter. Penelope saw the acknowledgment in her mother's eyes, that things had changed and would never be the same again.

When Penelope sat down at the end of the bed, her mother got up and left the room for the first time in two days. Dynah's gaze swept back and forth incredulously between the two of them, and then she too sat down, on the other side of the bed. Penelope opened the pouch of herbs and took out the cedar bark.

"Go make a tea with this," she told her sister.

Dynah nodded and went to the kitchen, and Penelope placed the sage in a metal cup on the bedside table and lit it with flame from the candle burning there. The sweet smoke began to waft up into the air. She strode around the room, letting it purify the toxic air. When Dynah returned with the tea a few minutes later, she wrinkled her nose but kept her mouth shut. They dribbled the tea slowly into Roy's mouth. After, they sat in silence for a long time. Their mother did not return, and Penelope heard her snores coming from the sitting room.

Finally, Dynah said, "What next?"

"We wait," Penelope answered.

CHAPTER TWENTY-THREE

Felicity

Felicity's mother had not recovered when the next music rehearsal came around a couple days after dinner with the preacher. She half expected her father to tell her she couldn't go alone, but he said nothing, and the church was only two blocks away from their house, after all.

She considered riding Music to practice, the thing a proper lady would do, but then, upon further reflection on the fact that no one had instructed her one way or another, Felicity chose to walk. Her boots were sturdy, and a little exercise never hurt anyone. So, a bit of dust from passing buggies would settle on her pale green dress and her pure white bonnet. Worse things could happen. A shiver of rebellion stirred inside her chest as she set out on her own.

The church was a large, plank-sided building. A sturdy gold-painted cross rose into the sky above it, and illuminated by the mid-afternoon sun, it spread radiance across the town. There had once been an attempt at growing grass in the yard, but the river ran a good distance away, and the unforgiving Colorado sun had long since shriveled the green blades into short brown spikes that looked like a strange fungus across the sandy earth. Felicity strode across it, her boots crunching with each step until she reached the wooden steps leading up to the door. She opened it and stepped inside. The single stained-glass window on the far side of the interior cast rainbow hues across the floor and up one wall.

"Felicity!" called Abigail. "So glad to see you."

Travis lifted a hand in greeting from his spot seated at the piano near the altar. Several other musicians nodded in greeting as she approached.

"Your mother couldn't make it?" the preacher asked.

"She's not feeling well."

"Sorry to hear that," he said. "I'm glad you could join us in spite of that."

"Happy to be here," she said with a shy bob of her head.

"Well, why don't you get warmed up while we wait on a couple more people?"

Felicity nodded and took a seat next to an enormous harp. It was bigger than the one she had at home, and not so finely tuned, but she played it often and her fingers found their rhythm almost instantly. Without her mother's penetrating gaze, she found she could focus much easier. She ran through the songs she would play at the fair, closing her eyes as the music moved through her, a vibration in her chest, in her bones, in her blood.

The other players arrived, and they worked through several songs together. After a while, Abigail asked Felicity to switch to the piano to play alongside Travis. He smiled as she joined him on the bench, and they practiced several new songs duet style. After they had warmed up and gotten accustomed to the close proximity of their bodies on the bench, and their hands playing the keys right next to each other, something of a silent competition formed between them. A subtle thing; one would play a challenging note to take the song to the next level and dart a glance over at the other. After a while, the rest of the players paused to watch them, and when at last they grew tired and cut off, laughing, the room filled with applause.

"That most certainly must be the finale of the fair!" someone called.

"I couldn't agree more," Abigail said.

"Back again tomorrow, same time?" the preacher said, looking around at everyone.

They all nodded in agreement and began to depart.

Felicity felt elation swell inside her. She finally fit in somewhere. Even Travis seemed to enjoy her company. How was it they'd gone to school and church together for so long and never spoken before? It had to be the music, she thought. She'd finally gotten a chance to play something she enjoyed. Not something her mother forced upon her. All that talk of shortcomings and failure, when the source of the whole thing was her predetermined disappointment. Felicity hoped, for a fleeting moment, that her mother never came to another practice.

"Goodnight, Felicity!" Travis called, heading out the back of the church with his mother.

The preacher stepped out front with a couple of the players, and for a moment Felicity found herself alone in the church. She realized she'd never actually stood there by herself. It was so rare she stood anywhere by herself, other than her brief escapes to the barn. She paused for a moment to relish the serenity of it, closing her eyes. Tasting her freedom.

A sound, the beating of wings, soft and somehow golden. Felicity opened her eyes, thinking a pigeon or a dove had made its way into the building. It wasn't a bird.

Tall, with silvery hair that brushed his shoulders, seeming to both absorb and reflect light off of it. His wings were golden, a soft, warm glow like candlelight, and he had brown skin like hers. A beam of blue light from the stained glass illuminated him, made him even more ethereal and impossible.

"Hello, Felicity," the angel said in a voice of moonlight and clear, flowing water.

She couldn't find words to respond.

"You're in shock. Understandable." He bowed his head

gracefully. "We don't have much time, however, and it's very important that we speak."

The angel seemed to radiate, to burn, like the light of a thousand stars. Felicity felt like all the world had fallen away except for her and the angel. Perhaps it had.

"What I'm about to tell you will be vital in the coming days. But I'm afraid you won't remember this conversation, not until you need to. Now hear my words…"

Felicity walked down Main Street. The sun shone brightly, and she'd had a lovely music practice at the church, and she was *happy*. It occurred to her how foreign and strange the emotion felt, because it visited her so seldomly.

She also realized she had no idea why she'd decided to walk down the street. She paused, feeling a sudden sense of unease, like she'd forgotten something. Why was she here? Why hadn't she gone back to her house after practice? Her mother would be furious if she found out.

But Felicity couldn't bring herself to care. She didn't have to have a reason to stroll down the street and enjoy the sun. She could walk through town without a destination. She could wander purposelessly like so many others. It made her feel a bit giddy.

And it was with that feeling bubbling up within her that she turned a corner and ran smack dab into Dynah Johnston.

Not a passing glance or graze of the shoulders, but a full-on collision. They both fell backwards onto the wooden walkway, almost as if propelled away from each other. Blinking in shock, Felicity looked at Dynah, and Dynah looked at Felicity.

"*You*," Dynah said. Something of awe and fear and curiosity rang in her voice.

And Felicity knew precisely what she meant. "From the dust storm. And the lightning strike. Yes."

They stared at each other again. Felicity's heart raced, and it wasn't from the jolt of falling and getting the wind knocked out of her. She reveled in Dynah's beauty, and it wasn't purely envy, not like the other women in town. Felicity was fairly certain none of the other women in town felt the way she felt about Dynah.

Dynah looked around as if suddenly realizing that sitting on the ground in the middle of town wasn't really appropriate. "Here. We can help each other up." She reached across to Felicity and grabbed both of her hands, and they used each other as counterweights to rise. A spark of electricity zinged between them.

"Hey, can we... talk? Somewhere private?" Dynah asked.

Felicity nodded, her words dying in her throat. They stepped into one of the alleys between buildings. Dynah looked back at the busy street, then lead them even further away from the hustle and bustle, until they stood in the shadows of an old distillery. There they stopped, and Dynah opened and closed her mouth a few times. Felicity waited for her to speak.

"I know I look a fright," Dynah said. "My father has been ill for days and I've barely left the house. But I had to pick up a few things for my mother." She patted the satchel at her side.

"You look… perfectly fine," Felicity managed. There was no reality in which Dynah wasn't gorgeous, although she could see purple rings under her eyes from lack of sleep. "I'm sorry about your father. I hope he's improving?"

Dynah nodded. "My sister—well, you probably know, I think everyone does—she's half Navajo. And she brought back some herbs from her tribe. They actually seem to be helping." She shrugged and smiled; it was the tired, delirious sort of smile of someone hanging on at the end of their rope.

Felicity nodded. "I'm glad to hear that." A pause. "So, what did you want to talk about?"

"Well," Dynah took a deep breath, let it hiss out between her lips. "Has anything… *strange*… happened to you? Since the dust storm?"

Felicity's eyes widened. Surely she was dreaming. Here she stood, speaking to the prettiest girl in town, someone she'd never imagined had even noticed her, and that same girl had asked the question that had haunted Felicity for the past week.

"Yes," she said. It rushed out of her mouth, breathy and desperate. "And you?"

Dynah nodded, a grimace twisting her face. "I thought at

first it was stress, because my father got sick and all, but it kind of started before that even."

"What kind of things happened?"

Dynah twirled a red curl around one finger. "Just… I don't know, seeing strange things. Odd *feelings*."

"Like the lightning is still moving around inside you?" Felicity whispered.

Another nod, tentative. "And seeing things that aren't there. I mean, that can't be there, you know?"

"Things just keep… *happening* around me," Felicity said, clasping her hands anxiously in front of her skirt.

"Yes," Dynah said. She let out a deep breath, a breath that seemed to carry all the weight of the world. "I'm so relieved it's not just me."

She reached out for Felicity's hand, and when their fingers touched, another electric spark shot between them. Both girls jerked back and looked down at their hands as if they were monsters. Slowly, Felicity reached out again. It happened a third time. She moved her hand back only a little, hovering her fingertips a couple of inches from Dynah's. That shimmering light, the light she'd only seen before when alone, moved across her skin and arced over to Dynah's hand. They stood there, feeling electricity move between them without even touching, watching the glow across their skin.

"How is this possible?" Dynah whispered.

"I don't know," Felicity said. Then, "Do you think the others have felt it, too?"

An odd look passed over Dynah's face, as if the thought occurred to her for the first time, and yet not. Like she realized something else. "I need to ask my sister," she said. "And Willow."

"Willow?"

Dynah's eyes widened. "The fourth person in the cyclone. She cut off her hair so no one would know a woman was entering the race. You can't tell anyone."

"I won't." Someone pretending to be a man was the least of Felicity's problems right now. The other secrets they kept were monumental in comparison. "So, what do we do now?"

"I need to get back to my house, check on my father," Dynah said. "I'll ask my sister if she's noticed anything. Let's meet back here tomorrow. The traveling merchants should all be setting up down by the arena."

"Three o'clock?" Felicity suggested. "By the arena?"

"It's a date," Dynah said.

Then she turned and strode off down the alley, leaving Felicity alone. Felicity felt relief and hope in her heart. She bowed her head in a quick prayer of thanks and was about to follow Dynah back to the street when she heard something behind her.

Spinning, her eyes searched the shadows at the end of the alley. If anyone had heard them... *seen* them...

Another rustle. Felicity strode forward, though fear clawed at her insides.

Then she spotted them.

Skeletons. That's what she thought they were at first. But they moved, and she realized in horror that they were people. Living, flesh and blood. So famished they looked like something from the grave.

As her eyes took them in, she experienced another jolt of shock. She recognized the two people on the ground, huddled next to a pile of broken barrels. The man and the woman who had tried to rob them. Tried to steal Music and their saddles and bridles.

She remembered what she had screamed at them that day: *"You don't know the meaning of* true *hunger."*

Well now, clearly, they did.

And Felicity knew that she had somehow caused this.

She doubled over and retched against the wall of the old distillery. Then she turned, stumbling, and fled the alley. She didn't look back.

CHAPTER TWENTY-FOUR

Dynah

When Dynah got back to the house, the doctor was there checking on her father. She put Moon in the barn, then hurried inside. Penelope sat in the living room as their mother spoke with the doctor. Dynah poked her head inside her parents' bedroom door.

"He's doing a lot better than he was yesterday," the doctor said, looking up at her mother from where he bent over her father with his stethoscope. "Not out of the woods yet, but I'd say it's looking positive."

Her mother crossed herself and looked up, murmuring a prayer of thanks. Dynah could still see the dark aura around the doctor, but it had faded to a smoke-gray. She looked over at Penelope, who stared back stoically.

"And you say you've been using these herbs?" The doctor

asked.

Dynah stepped out of the bedroom and gestured for Penelope to follow her outside. Penelope gave her a questioning look but did as requested. They went out through the front door and around the corner of their house. Dynah stopped in the shadows at the back, where cobwebs clung to the eaves of the roof. She turned to face Penelope.

"What's going on?" Penelope asked.

"I need to ask you something," Dynah said. But now that it came down to it, reluctance made her balk. Their relationship was just so… complicated. It had been easier to talk to Felicity, a complete stranger. "The other day… the dust storm," Dynah began. "It was strange, right?"

Penelope stared at her, silent.

"I mean, the lightning? How we were all unharmed?"

Something moved behind Penelope's eyes this time. Dynah pushed forward. "Has anything else… odd… been happening to you since then?"

"Like what?" Penelope finally said.

The front door opened and the sound of the doctor's voice could be heard. Their mother called them to fetch his horse. "I'll show you," Dynah whispered, and she gestured for Penelope to follow her again.

They went to the barn, and Dynah got the doctor's horse out of one of the stalls. She led the gelding around to the front of the house. As they approached, Dynah leaned over to Penelope and whispered, "Watch the doctor."

Penelope shot her a look but kept her mouth shut. Dynah handed the reins over to the doctor and waved farewell as he mounted up and rode off down the dirt road. She could see the ghostly gray outline shifting around him the whole time.

After he rode out of earshot, Dynah turned to her sister. "Did you see it?"

"See what?"

Dynah felt her heart sink. Maybe her sister hadn't experienced the same things that she and Felicity had.

"Listen, Dynah," Penelope said, her voice low and tense. "I don't know what you're trying to pull here, but I don't appreciate it. I came back here, all the way from the Navajo reservation, because Willow said you needed me. But you've barely spoken to me since then, and now you're suddenly asking me cryptic questions."

"No, I'm serious," Dynah said, not liking how whiny her voice sounded. "I'm—I'm seeing things. Ever since that day at the arena. The doctor—he had this strange cloud around him. It was black the other day, but now it's gray—"

"Is this a joke?" Penelope growled. "It wasn't enough that you summoned me back here like the servant you all think I am. Now you have to taunt me?"

"What? No!" Dynah cried. "We don't think you're a servant. Don't be silly."

"I have *never* been treated like a member of this family,"

Penelope spat. "Least of all by Roy."

"Oh, so you're glad he got sick?"

"That's not what I said! I would never wish that."

"Well, he got sick right after your big fight the other day. Within hours. Don't you think that's bizarre?"

Penelope's eyes widened. "You think *I* caused Roy's illness? How would I even do that?"

Dynah clenched and unclenched her fists at her sides. This was not at all how she'd imagined the conversation going. "I don't—I just—I told you, things have been strange lately—"

"Why don't you do us both a favor and go back to ignoring me like you usually do." Penelope spat out the words, then turned and stormed off into the woods.

Dynah let out a groan of frustration and walked back into the house. The whole place smelled of sage, which just reminded her of Penelope and her new family once again. How could she say they treated her like a servant? Not a member of the family? Maybe Penelope had never wanted to be a part of their family. She'd left the first chance she got, and she'd probably be out of here again as soon as Roy recovered.

It was true she hadn't spoken much to Penelope since she came back a couple days before. They'd never been close. They didn't make idle chit-chat with each other, as many sisters did, it just wasn't like that between them. Plus, Dynah didn't know how to ask about Penelope's Navajo family, and she'd been trying to muster the courage to talk about what had happened since the dust storm. Which had clearly been a complete failure when she finally did get the words out.

The only upside to things was that her father seemed to have a fighting chance now. She wouldn't have to cancel her entry in the rodeo anymore, as she'd been contemplating. Death had steered clear of their household.

Things could finally get back to normal.

CHAPTER TWENTY-FIVE

Willow

Willow had agreed, against her better judgment, to meet Zane for a picnic. They still had to practice for the race, as he'd accurately pointed out, and that required eating along the way. Why not eat together?

As she approached their rendezvous point, she felt as if she'd swallowed several large fuzzy caterpillars, which now gnawed on her insides. Was this what romance felt like? Because if so, she now knew why it hadn't been an interest to her thus far. What she *didn't* know was why she wanted so badly to see him even so.

Damn it all.

Zane sat waiting for her on the boulder. It was a couple miles south of her house, along the river. She'd told him he couldn't miss it. A boulder so big, either a giant or God could have been the only ones to place it there, oddly out of place in the open plains south of the red rock canyons. The late afternoon sun painted everything gold.

Willow let Bullet loose to graze with Zane's horse, taking off her bridle so she could eat freely. She'd had the chestnut mare long enough to know she wouldn't wander off. She tossed her bridle on a smaller rock next to the giant boulder and climbed up to meet Zane.

"I thought for a bit you were going to stand me up," he said by way of greeting.

Willow blinked. "Am I that late?"

He chuckled. "Just a bit. Thought maybe I spooked you off. Figuring out your secret and all."

"I'm not so easily spooked," Willow said with a shrug.

She sat down next to him. Not too close. The boulder was more or less flat on the top, so they had plenty of room. But then she started to wonder if she'd sat oddly far from him. She groaned inwardly. It had been much easier being a man.

"I brought sandwiches," Zane said, holding up a small package wrapped in brown paper. "Roast beef. Hope that's okay."

"Yeah, thanks." Willow lifted a small burlap sack. "Apples. Last of the Fall harvest. A bit wrinkly but still sweet." She pulled one out and tossed it over.

Zane smiled. "Thanks." He took a bite of the red-gold fruit, and a bit of the juice ran down his chin. "So, how many miles did you go today?"

"Thirty, give or take. You?"

"About the same. With the race in two days, I want Jericho to be fresh. Just a light jog the next couple days."

Willow nodded. "That was my plan, too."

She sat back and took a bite of her sandwich. The bread was thick and fresh, the meat salty. She hadn't realized how hungry she was until now. Maybe this picnic wasn't the worst idea in the world. They were talking about the race. It didn't mean Zane liked her in any kind of way. And she didn't have to feel anything particular in return. Just two riders sharing a meal and talking about their jobs.

Zane pulled a silver flask out of his back pocket and took a swig, then tossed it over to her. Willow caught it with her free hand. As she raised it to her lips, she caught the sharp tang of whiskey, so strong it made her eyes water. What had Lyla said before she left? No boys, no guns, no booze, and don't forget to feed the chickens? Willow tipped the flask into her mouth, making sure not to wince as the liquid burned down her throat. Well. She hadn't forgotten to feed the chickens.

She tossed the whiskey back to Zane and polished off her sandwich, then the apple. Zane scooted closer to her so he could hand her the flask this time, instead of tossing it from the other side of the boulder. She took another gulp, and this time the heat lingered in her chest. It was actually a pleasant sensation, a spreading warmth that swam through her veins.

"So, about our alliance," Zane said.

"Yeah?" Willow handed the flask back to him.

"I think it might be compromised."

She stiffened, then narrowed her eyes. "How so?"

"Well, it was easy when I didn't know you." Zane took a pull from the flask. "Because then I wouldn't have any problem beating you, in the end."

"Ha." Willow snorted, took the flask back. "That's awfully arrogant." She held his eyes as she took another sip of whiskey.

"True," he said. "But my point is, now I think I would feel bad if I won."

"Really? Because if you somehow manage to beat me—which there's just the tiniest, infinitesimal chance of—you should be very proud of yourself. It would be quite the feat."

"Now who's arrogant?" Zane grinned and took the flask back.

Willow felt very warm and happy now. No wonder men liked whiskey so much. "The problem here, Zane, is that you're viewing me as a woman."

His brow wrinkled. "Well. You are that."

She raised a hand. "For the purposes of the race, I have chosen to be a man. You weren't supposed to figure it out, but you did. So, there's a simple solution."

"And what's that?"

"Just treat me like any other cowboy. Forget entirely that I am, in fact, a woman."

"Hmm," he said.

Willow abruptly realized that Zane was sitting quite close to her.

When had that happened? It had to be all the passing back and forth of the flask. She sat cross-legged, and his long legs stretched out next to hers, their thighs almost touching. Their shoulders were inches apart, too. She could smell him even, his leather-sage scent.

"Forget you're a woman?" he repeated. "I don't think that's going to be possible."

He reached out one hand and brushed his pinky finger delicately along the top of her hand where it sat resting on her knee. Willow felt a heat flare up between them that had nothing to do with the whiskey. Zane's river blue eyes burned into her jade ones.

"Well then," she said breathily. "Maybe you should just forfeit now."

He leaned in toward her, brushed a strand of hair off her cheek. Then closer, until their breath mingled and she could hear his heart thumping. His lips hovered above hers. "I forfeit," he whispered.

A shrill whinny broke the air and they looked up to see a group of cowboys riding toward them. Cowboys who of course thought that Willow was a boy. And while she thought two cowboys could do and feel whatever they wanted for each other, she doubted very much that sentiment would be carried by the rough-riders coming up on them.

Zane scooted back hastily before they got too close, then raised a hand in greeting. "Howdy."

The men raised hands in greeting as they passed by. Jericho and Bullet, excited by the new horses, went trotting off toward them. "Shit!" Willow said.

They shimmied off the boulder and went after them. It didn't take long to capture the two runaways, as they were both pretty worn out from their earlier rides. Willow was more than a bit relieved the group of riders passed on by without incident. She remembered the ambush in the canyon all too well.

"That was close," she said, watching them head north toward Hawk's Hollow.

"Yeah."

Zane looked over, and those blue eyes almost undid her. It *had* been close. Too close.

"I'd better lay low the next couple of days," Willow said. "I'd hate to have come this far only to blow my cover right before the race."

"You're right." Zane nodded. "I don't want that, either."

"Listen," she said. "It's nearly the turn of the century. A man and a woman can compete against each other. No hard feelings, no matter who wins the race, eh?"

"Deal," he said. "No feelings of any kind until after the race."

"Agreed," Willow said. "Good."

She reached out her hand, he grabbed it, and they shook.

Willow swung up onto Bullet, feeling a little unsteady as she did. Part of it was the whiskey. But the other part…

"Thanks for the sandwiches," she said.

Zane shrugged. "Of course. So, see you on race day?"

Willow picked up her reins and straightened her hat on her head. "See you on race day."

CHAPTER TWENTY-SIX

Since Roy clearly wasn't dying anymore, Penelope was of half a mind to head right back out to her clan again and leave Dynah and her mother to fend for themselves. After all, they'd always left her on her own. An outsider in her own family. But, as eager as she felt to get back to Nascha and Atsa and learn more about the other half of her, there was one thing she needed to do first.

Enter the rodeo.

Her last act of defiance. Well, one of her only acts of defiance, after a life of being quiet and staying out of the way. Of acting like she had to atone for the blood running through her veins. Roy had forbidden her to enter the rodeo. Well, her Navajo side had saved his life, so as far as she figured, he didn't have a leg to stand on. And Dynah... well, her sister would just have to get over having a little competition.

Penelope saddled Domino and headed for town. It was early morning, but the sun already baked the earth. She longed for the crisp mornings of autumn, when dew still clung to blades of grass, when the shadows made you shiver. When stepping out of the house didn't suck the energy right out of you.

When she reached Hawk's Hollow, the whole place was abuzz with activity. With the fair starting tomorrow, nearly everyone from out of town had arrived by now, and it was packed. The hotel sold out, the saloon overflowing, the land between the train station and the arena, a good half-mile, completely lined with traveling merchants, and beyond that, tents for the folk who couldn't afford a hotel room. Penelope figured an extra few hundred people descended on her little town for the annual fair.

She rode down Main Street and watched the bustle, then cut over at the south end of town to the fairgrounds. It was even more packed than the street had been. Domino pranced, feeling the excitement in the air. They made their way to the line for the registration table. There had to be a couple dozen people ahead of her. She tried not to be discouraged—she had nowhere else she needed to be at the moment.

The minutes passed, and the sun beat down on her. Penelope began to sweat, feeling it dampen her brown cotton blouse. It felt like everyone was staring at her. Maybe the out-of-towners were surprised to see a brown girl in line for the rodeo. She stared right back at anyone with lingering eyes. Her days of meekness were behind her.

She finally reached the head of the line and got off Domino. "I'd like to register for the rodeo. Trick riding."

The two men before her were the same ones that had been there that fated day of the dust storm. "I'm sorry," said the one, "But you're going to need Roy's permission to enter."

Penelope stiffened. "I'm eighteen. An adult."

They shrugged.

Penelope could feel her skin getting hot, and tingles running along her collarbone. "But my sister didn't need Roy's permission to enter!"

"Sorry," said the second cowboy in the most unapologetic way possible.

Lightning coursed through Penelope's veins. Always, this same treatment. As if she weren't a citizen of this town. As if she weren't a *human being*. She felt her anger glow within her, and then it surged out of her eyes and into the first cowboy who had spoken, who stared at her balefully. He stiffened a moment, then began to cough. The other man clapped him on the back, which only seemed to intensify the hacking.

Penelope turned her burning gaze to the second man…

"I think perhaps I can resolve this situation," said a voice behind her. A female voice.

Penelope turned and the lightning faded. A woman stepped up next to her. Tall, pale as ice, with a pile of ebony curls atop her head, and an emerald green fascinator that matched her eyes. She wore a pink and bone-colored satin dress with a corset. A leather sheath hung around her waist, carrying a jeweled dagger. She leaned, ever so slightly, on a frilly, folded parasol.

She was definitely not from Hawk's Hollow.

"I'll pay the young lady's entry fee," said the woman. She dropped a handful of gold coins on the table and slid them across to the men. They weren't dollar coins, but something older, from across the sea.

The first one still coughed, but the second man stared at the woman with huge eyes, looked back down at the pile of coins, then hastily began to write Penelope's information on the roster. After a moment, he ripped off a receipt and handed it to Penelope with shaking fingers. She took it and stepped out of line, leading Domino behind her.

She turned to her savior. "Thank you so much. Why did you…?"

The woman smiled, and her pink lips glistened in the sun like freshly cut watermelon. "Us women have to stick together, don't you think?" She winked at Penelope as they continued to walk through the crowd.

"That's true," Penelope said, glancing over at the dazzling woman. "But most people don't want to help me."

"Why ever not?" The woman said, looking over at her in surprise.

"Well, you know…" Penelope drifted off, looking down at

her brown arms.

"I can't imagine what you mean." The woman paused, the skirts of her ostentatious dress swirling around her booted ankles. "Remember this: there will always be people who want to hold you back. It's up to you to take what you know is yours."

And with that, the woman opened her parasol to shield her from the sun, smiled a smile both sweet and sharp, and sauntered away into the crowd. Penelope stood there in awe and in shock, watching as the woman disappeared amongst the milling cowboys.

CHAPTER TWENTY-SEVEN

Felicity

Felicity didn't think she'd ever been more anxious in her entire life, and that was saying a lot. It was 2:58 PM. She stood by the arena, waiting for the prettiest girl in the world, waiting, of all things, to talk about strange forces that had affected them both since that fateful day two weeks ago in this very place.

She had to be dreaming.

A huge crowd surrounded the arena. She sat on Music, patting her sleek black shoulder from time to time to calm her from the commotion. How on earth would she and Dynah even find each other in all these people? Felicity cursed inwardly. She should have thought about that when they'd arranged a meeting place. Now it was too late.

And then she felt something… a bit like the lightning

flowing in her veins. The white light glimmered from her hands, and Felicity was glad she'd worn her riding gloves so it only peeked out around the edges. She felt a tug in her gut, in her blood, and she looked to the west. Across the crowd, beyond the arena toward Main Street, she saw Dynah emerge from the milling bodies on her pale horse.

She urged Music forward and they made their way through the throng. West, toward Dynah, but also south just a bit to a less crowded area between the arena and the row of traveling merchants. Dynah seemed to beeline in her direction, and they met out in the open behind the tents of the peddlers.

"Hi," Dynah said, and for once she seemed shy, unsure of herself. Not the confident Rodeo Queen everyone knew and loved. She pulled her horse alongside Music so they faced each other.

"Hello," Felicity answered.

"I didn't know how I was going to find you," Dynah said, then paused. "But then—I—I kind of—"

"Felt my location?" Felicity finished.

Dynah nodded, her eyes widening. "What is happening to us?" Her voice came out a whisper.

"I wish I knew." They looked at each other a moment. "Your sister isn't coming?"

Dynah's face darkened. "She didn't seem to know what I was talking about. We got in an argument."

"Oh," Felicity said. She felt both surprised and strangely...

satisfied. Maybe she and Dynah alone shared these powers. "I'm sorry to hear that."

A shrug. "My sister and I—we don't see eye to eye on a lot of things. Nothing new there." She sounded sad, though, which belied the gesture.

"How is your father doing?"

"Much better," Dynah said. "It seems he's going to pull through."

"Well, that's wonderful news!" Felicity smiled.

"Yes. I'm so relieved."

Silence fell between them. After several long moments, Felicity said, "So, what do we do? Should we try to talk to Willow?"

Dynah made a face. "She doesn't like me much. I'm afraid I might get a similar reaction from her."

Felicity wasn't sure what to say next. Where did they go from here?

Movement on her periphery caught her attention. She turned her head to see a woman step out of one of the merchant's tents not far off. The woman stared in their direction and then gestured for them to come over. Or at least, it seemed she did. Felicity looked over her shoulder to see if the woman was signaling someone else.

Dynah followed her gaze. "What are you looking at?"

"That woman." Felicity pointed, then ducked her head when she realized her rudeness in doing so. "It looked like she waved for us to come over."

"She probably wants to sell us something."

They both turned back to the woman, who gestured for them again. She appeared to be a fortune teller or something of that sort. The type of woman that Felicity's mother always warned her about: wavy black hair held back in a colorful scarf, a long red dress, lots of jewelry. Felicity's mother said women who dressed like that cavorted with demons.

"I don't know. Fortune tellers are known for their knowledge of the supernatural. I think we should go see," Felicity said, surprised at her own boldness. "After all, what do we have to lose?"

"You do have a point," Dynah said, though she looked dubious.

Felicity didn't wait for her to change her mind. She nudged Music forward. Dynah followed on her gray and they approached the back of the woman's tent. The fortune teller stood waiting for them, the flap of her tent held open.

"I can sense fellow women in need," she said, her dark eyes grazing over each of them. Her voice sounded of smoke and steel.

They tied the horses to a post at the back of the tent and stepped inside. It was not the sort of place Felicity's mother would have approved of in the least. And there was also, undeniably, some sort of magic afoot.

For starters, the tent looked four times as large on the inside.

What appeared from the outside to be a small, ordinary tent now soared over their heads, spacious and grand. A cluster of colored glass lanterns hung from the apex, emitting thin curls of herbaceous smoke. On the left side of the tent, against the wall, stood an altar covered entirely in black crystals. Mirroring it on the right side stood an altar holding clear crystals. Two bay horses stood on one side of the tent, snoozing in a circle of flickering candles. Feathers and colored threads and beads were braided into their manes and tails. Thick, woven rugs carpeted the ground. Near the front of the tent stood a table and two chairs.

The fortune teller eyed Felicity. "You can see it all, can't you?"

Felicity nodded, as did Dynah, whose eyes were wide as she took everything in.

"I knew there was something about you girls," the woman said with a wave of her hand. "I am Davania. What do I call you by?"

Felicity introduced herself first, offering her hand and dipping into a brief curtsy, but the fortune teller simply touched a knuckle to her forehead. "I cannot touch your skin until I am ready to see everything."

Dynah frowned and looked over at Felicity before sharing her name as well.

Davania led the way to the table and chairs in the front of the room. With a wave of her hand, one of the chairs duplicated, and now three chairs stood before them. Davania smiled as she took in the astonished expressions of the two girls.

"You already saw through my glamour," she said. "No point hiding anything, eh?"

Felicity sat down and folded her hands neatly in her lap, realizing that her life up to this point made her vastly unprepared for the strange things happening to her now. She became overly conscious of her spotlessly clean lavender dress and the white bonnet strapped over her hair. The tiny golden cross over her heart, beneath the tight buttons running all the way up to the base of her chin.

"What's a glamour?" she blurted out. She really had no idea what was happening, and things were so far beyond her ken she feared she'd never get back to normalcy again.

Davania looked at her, really *looked* at her good and long. Felicity thought she could see swirls of something moving in the dark depths of the woman's eyes.

"It is a spell I put on my tent to make it seem…to meet expectations," she said. "Normal folk want to see a humble fortune teller with little in the way of personal belongings. They want to see a little pizzazz, but nothing too far outside of their comfort zone."

"A spell…" Dynah murmured. "Like, a magic spell?"

Davania looked at Dynah now, as she had looked at Felicity. And Dynah, who no doubt had been stared at every day of her whole life, fidgeted beneath the gaze.

"Magic," the woman said, and her lips curled around the word like a lover. "The two of you have been touched by it as well. That's what I felt when I invited you inside. That's why you can see through my glamour without even trying. But neither of you seem to know the first thing about it." She cackled then, as if it were funny.

"Can you help us, then?" Felicity asked.

"I don't have much money on me," Dynah said.

Davania waved a hand. "I charge the sheep who live in the towns I visit. I do not charge fellow women touched by the mysteries."

The woman reached her hand out across the table between them, palm up. "I will look now. Who will go first?" She issued it like a challenge, a dare. But then a shiver went over her, and she shook her head. "No. Both, together. Your fates are intertwined."

Felicity looked over at Dynah, whose blue eyes seemed to glow in the dim lighting of the tent. Dynah nodded, and in unison, they reached out to touch the fortune teller's hand.

CHAPTER TWENTY-EIGHT

Dynah

Dynah and Felicity's fingers touched the weathered palm of the fortune teller, and the woman stiffened as if zapped with electricity. Her eyes looked through them, beyond them, into something Dynah couldn't see.

Davania opened her mouth and spoke, but her voice had changed, deepened, as if it came from the earth below them, deeper even, from the roots at the center of the earth, from the dark places where sunlight did not reach. "Two of the four, four of the four."

A brisk wind picked up inside the tent, swirling the smoke, making the horses snort and shimmy in place.

"The four shall ride... and darkness follows...darkness and fire and wings...wings...wings..."

Davania jerked again and her eyes rolled back in her head. Felicity squeaked, her eyes wide with horror. Dynah could only imagine a similar look marred her own features.

Then it was over, and Davania was Davania again. She jerked her hand back from the girls.

"What did you see?" Dynah asked, her voice shaking. She didn't want to know, not really, but the words escaped her mouth before she could stop them.

Several long moments passed before the fortune teller answered. "Things I have never seen before. Things I have never even dreamed of. And I have seen *nightmares*." She shivered in remembrance of whatever she referred to.

And then, abruptly, she stood. "I need to be going. I will see you two out."

"Wait, what?" Felicity stammered. "Tell us what you saw. We need help."

Davania drew in a deep breath, pulling herself up tall as she did so. "I am not sure that I can offer you anything to help, child. I help ward away evil. It is much harder when evil has already taken hold."

Dynah felt like she'd been slapped in the face. "Us? You're saying we're evil?"

In her mind she saw the black aura around the doctor, felt the call of the dead in the graveyard. She knew the truth already. Something inside her began to crumble. The careful control of her life, which she kept in a deadly grip behind her bright smile, a constant tension no one ever saw or knew.

Davania cocked her head to the side. "I see the world burning in your eyes. It's already begun."

Felicity sucked in a sharp breath, and Dynah saw a tear trickle down her cheek.

"However," the fortune teller said. "We all have a choice. Darkness may be sitting at your dinner table, but you don't have to share a meal."

"I don't understand," Dynah whispered. She could feel her own tears stinging the corners of her eyes, and she dug her fingernails into her palms.

"There will come a time. Soon. Your choice will have to be made." Davania made a gesture in the air before her, like a spiral.

The fortune teller walked to the back of the tent and lifted the flap for them. Felicity looked like a beaten dog as she walked toward her, head bowed. Davania frowned, looking as if she debated something in her head, then dropped the tent flap and walked over to her horses. She took a single brown feather from the tail of each, one hung from a black thread, one from a silver-gray. She handed the black one to Felicity, and the gray one to Dynah.

"Those might help. A little. To help you remember who you are." The woman opened the tent flap once more. "I'm sorry to deliver such terrible news."

Felicity nodded and stepped out of the tent. Dynah followed, but when she reached Davania, she stopped. "Where will you go?"

Davania's mouth tightened. "As far from Hawk's Hollow as I can travel." And she dropped the tent flap in Dynah's face.

Dynah untied Moon's reins from the post, fingers trembling. Her thoughts spun as if swirled with snow, growing colder and slower with each moment. She was going into shock and she knew it. Simply too much to process at one time.

They walked a few dozen paces beyond the tent before Felicity finally spoke. "I'm sorry."

Dynah turned. "What?"

"You didn't want to go, but I thought we should, and—well, it was awful." She sniffled and wiped her nose on her white gloves in a very unladylike gesture. "What do you think she meant by all that?"

"I don't know," Dynah said softly. The ice moved into her bloodstream now, winter taking over her lungs, her heart. Quiet. Dark. Felicity was saying something else, but she couldn't make out the words.

"Dynah!" someone yelled. A male someone.

She looked up to see Billy. Golden-haired Billy. Golden like the sun. He stood off behind the arena with a few friends.

"There's my favorite Rodeo Queen!" He waved. "Come over here!"

And Dynah wanted his warmth. She needed it, or else this chill inside of her would consume everything. Davania had said she had a choice to make, and this was it: she didn't have to believe a *damn* word of any of this. She would go back to living her normal life. She would forget the blackness and the dead and the feeling of lightning running through her veins. She would make herself forget.

Which meant one thing for certain.

"Bye, Felicity," she said.

The other girl's doe eyes widened. "Don't we need to talk about this? About what just happened?"

Dynah jerked her head from side to side decisively. "No. I think we should both do our very best to forget about it. That lady was clearly a quack."

"But the windstorm, the strange happenings, the sparks…"

"Just leave it alone," Dynah said, and she could hear the whiplash in her tone. "That's what I'm going to do. I suggest you do the same."

She turned then, leaving Felicity agape behind her, eyes shimmering with tears, and she left the winter behind her.

CHAPTER TWENTY-NINE

Willow

The devil himself couldn't have asked for a hotter day. Even at eight o'clock in the morning the sun burned furiously, vindictively. A sadistic jailer torturing its captives.

Willow couldn't have been happier.

Race day had finally arrived, and nothing on this earth could keep her from it. From her victory. Her ticket out of Hawk's Hollow. Her escape route into a new life.

Bullet pranced beneath her, and a hot wind kissed her skin. About two dozen other riders lined up next to them, all in a row. They stood a few paces from the arena, facing west. The mayor of Hawk's Hollow, a squat little man with a handlebar mustache, stood on the wooden stage at the head of the arena. Pretty much the whole town had gathered, along with travelers from far and wide. Everyone came to see the start of the race. It kicked off the three days of the annual fair, competitions in every form between horse and rider. An unrivaled moment each and every year.

And this was *her* year.

"Riders, are you ready?" called the mayor.

A chorus of yells and hats flung into the air answered him.

"On your marks, gentlemen!"

And lady, Willow thought with a swell of excitement in her gut. Next to her on his buckskin, Zane shot her a look that made her insides burn.

"Get set!"

The mayor raised his Remington pistol overhead. Bullet was a thunderclap beneath her, about to explode. Willow's heart pounded hard enough to crack her ribcage.

"Go! And good luck!"

The pistol fired into the sky, a crack that split the clouds. Bullet let loose beneath her, true to her namesake, shooting out across the plains. The wind whipped in Willow's eyes, across her cheeks, and poured down her throat. She nearly lost her hat as they tore across the wide yonder. She couldn't see any other horses in her periphery; Bullet had jumped out ahead of them all. Willow felt her heart soar into the sky above them.

She was free.

They kept their lead for a mile before Willow slowed Bullet to a lope, then a trot. This race was about endurance. She and

Bullet could both run forever, run until they died, but that wouldn't win the thing. And win it she would. She imagined Penelope's surprised face at her incredible restraint, and that made her smile.

Zane pulled up alongside her, his gelding nosing Bullet, which elicited a squeal of protest from the mare. "That was some sprint."

Willow patted Bullet's sweaty neck. "She bears her name for a reason."

"Well, I'd better move off. Don't want the other cowboys to think we have an arrangement or something." Zane grinned and veered off into the plains.

The miles passed and so did the hours. Nothing but red earth, blue sky, puffs of cloud like gun smoke, and the occasional eagle high above. Willow alternated between trotting and cantering, stopping at any creeks they passed (there weren't many) to let Bullet get water and to refill her water skin.

Morning slipped away into afternoon. Afternoon slid toward evening. Red buttes rose up from the desert floor like ancient warriors stretching between earth and the sky. Willow caught an occasional far-off glimpse of another cowboy, but she was mostly alone. Well, alone except for Bullet. She'd heard more than enough tales of the tricks and outright cheating some of these men would resort to in an attempt to knock out the competition. Their suspicion kept big swaths of space between them.

Of course, out here in the open there wasn't a whole lot you could do other than shoot someone. Cactuses provided the only cover. But once they swung north and hit the mountains, an abundance of opportunities for sabotage revealed themselves. Rockslides. Downed trees. Soured water. And ambushes, of course, which Willow was all too familiar with.

Before the mountains, however, she had to reach Devil's Eye Peak, the western checkpoint. It stood at the halfway point, fifty miles from Hawk's Hollow. The northern checkpoint would be reached on the second day, and sat roughly halfway back to town. The rules were simple: it didn't matter how you got there and how you got back. But they had to see you at those checkpoints in order to claim victory.

Willow planned to hit the first checkpoint before nightfall, then head up into the mountains. It would be tricky after the sun set, and sabotage would be all the easier to accomplish, but she'd have to slow down in the mountains, which required some travel after dark if she wanted to ensure her win. That's where her Colt came in handy. Any cowboy who tried to cheat would meet the business end of her iron real fast.

The sun was melting like candlewax toward the horizon as Willow arrived at Devil's Eye Peak, a huge red butte that jutted up from the desert floor like a medieval fortress. Two men sat in the back of a covered wagon at the base of it.

"Will Bullet," she said to them.

One of the cowboys wrote her name on a piece of brown

paper. She glanced down and saw that it was blank otherwise.

"I'm the first one to come through?"

"Yes'sir," said the one.

"But don't get cocky," said another. "Tomorrow will be harder."

They took a clockwork raven from the wagon, which Willow recognized as Harvey's handiwork, and placed another scrap of paper bearing her name in a compartment in its mouth. Then they wound it up and released it towards Hawk's Hollow. Willow imagined the raven arriving at the arena, the crowd waiting in excitement as the mayor opened the message and read her name aloud. She'd been one of those people in the crowd each year before, remembered the palpable thrill of each name being called. Now it was *her* name.

She tipped her hat to the cowboys and galloped off. So far, so good. Everything was going according to plan. Victory hovered so close she could taste the metallic tang of it on her tongue.

Naturally, that's when the storm started to roll in.

Willow could tell it was going to be a bad one. Dark clouds, nearly black, stampeding like buffalo across the sky. The wind picked up, and in the distance, she could see flashes of lightning strike a couple buttes. The mountains were three miles off at least. Would it be better to be out in the open when the storm caught her, or find shelter? It was hard to choose such things when contending with Mother Nature.

She decided to make for the mountains. Even if she didn't make it, or even if she couldn't find a safe, high place out of the way of flash floods and the like, she wanted to gain as many miles as she could before the storm forced her to slow down. They didn't have extra time to waste.

Bullet accelerated across the plains. They raced the storm now, a competition apart from the cowboys. Horse, woman, lightning, thunder. Raw energy, streaking across the wide-open. Rebels against the wind. When the rain started to pelt them, it felt like gunfire, hot and sharp. Nothing matched the fury of a summer storm, with all its pent-up heat and frustration.

They were soaked to the bone in less than a minute. Willow lost sight of the mountains as a curtain of driving rain swept down in front of them. The downpour extinguished the last rays of the sun. Darkness raged around them.

Willow slowed Bullet to a walk. She couldn't see shit and she wasn't going to risk her horse. The footing was soup as well, sucking at them, hungry. Willow turned her face down, letting her hat take the force of the rain. She patted Bullet's neck to comfort her. And they walked on.

A few minutes later Willow heard hoofbeats. She turned, but she still couldn't see a thing. She thought she heard a horse neigh to her left, but the wind howled like a banshee and she couldn't be sure.

Then he was there in the darkness on his buckskin. Zane. Drenched, as Willow was, his black hair plastered to his face.

Thunder clapped overhead and a bolt of purple lightning kissed the ground not a hundred yards away, illuminating everything around them, sending a jolt of energy through Willow's veins. And just for a moment, in the flash, she thought Zane had wings.

Their eyes met. Willow wasn't sure what it was. The race, the storm. The heat from the lightning. The fragility of life in that moment. She swung her leg over Bullet's neck and dismounted in one smooth movement; Zane kicked out of his stirrups and did the same. Their eyes never left each other's as they took two strides and came together with all the power and urgency of the maelstrom pounding around them.

Willow snaked her hand around the back of Zane's neck, and he grabbed her hips with both hands. They crushed the space between them. Thighs touching, hearts beating against each other. Lips hungry and searching. Zane was her oxygen, and Willow devoured him. And it still wasn't enough.

She tugged at his shirt, snatching at the buttons, and he did the same with hers. It took a moment, in the torrential rain, but she finally managed to tug it off. Zane threw it off into the darkness somewhere. Her shirt came next, and then she turned in a slow circle as he unwound the binding around her chest.

Belts came next, tossed into the mud, jeans yanked down, boots flung off. Until it was only them, bare beneath the force of nature. The wind and the rain and the fire in the sky. Lightning struck again, closer this time, and the earth shook.

They looked at each other in the brilliance. Willow trembled in awe and in fear and in pleasure.

Then, she tugged Zane to the earth with her, and they created their own glorious storm.

CHAPTER THIRTY

Penelope

Penelope had seen Willow start the race that morning and then spent the rest of the day watching the rodeo. The trick riding wasn't until the second day, so she'd had all day to get her stomach tied in knots.

Luckily, bronco riding proved to somewhat distract her from her nerves. Mustangs brought from all over the state, some even from as far as Wyoming. Chestnuts and bays, grays and Appaloosas. A couple stunning paints and buckskins. They looked different, but each had one thing in common: they were wild as hell. Hand-picked for the competition because of their unbreakable spirits.

It made Penelope sad to see them man-handled by the cowboys. But the horses seemed to take great pleasure in throwing one after another. Discovering new and extraordinary aerial feats off the ground. Stomping on the ones who didn't get out of the ring fast enough. It was thrilling and terrifying to watch.

Dynah had been there all day, too, though they hadn't spoken. Penelope wondered if her sister realized she'd signed up for the rodeo. If Dynah thought for a second that she would sit this one out, she was sadly mistaken. And with Roy mostly better, neither of them had to feel guilty about it. He'd been up this morning sitting at the dining room table when they'd left for the start of the race.

Penelope's eyes darted over to her sister, who seemed attached at the hip to Billy-the-brainless-cowboy. Dynah was laughing in that way that only her sister could laugh. Not a care in the world. Well, at least that's what everyone thought. What she herself had thought, until recently. But Dynah had been trying to tell her something when they'd fought the other day. About strange things happening since the dust cyclone. And as much as Penelope wanted to disregard it, she knew her sister was right.

A sigh escaped her lips. She'd been too angry the other day, but she needed to talk to Dynah about it. Tonight. She'd ask her sister to tell her everything, and then they'd figure something out. Penelope wanted to get back to her clan, and she couldn't do that if this was hanging over her head.

When late afternoon cast golden fingers of light over the arena, Penelope turned for home. She wanted to get in a practice session with Domino before the big event tomorrow, and she certainly wasn't going to do it here. She steered Domino over to where Dynah sat on Moon, surrounded by pretty much every boy their age.

"I'm headed home to practice," she called to her sister. "Why don't you join me?"

"Maybe in a bit," Dynah said.

"We need to talk," Penelope said in a tone that sent a clear message to her sister. They locked eyes a moment, then Penelope turned Domino and headed for home.

Dynah caught up to her a quarter-mile later. By this point, Penelope was passing Hawk's Hollow on the west side, heading north. The noise of the rodeo had fallen behind them. They rode in silence for a short while.

"About the other night," Penelope said finally. "You wanted to tell me something."

"You didn't seem interested," Dynah said.

She sounded prideful and prickly, but beneath it, Penelope detected an undernote of pain. She looked over at her sister. "I'm interested now."

Dynah remained silent for another minute, seeming to get up the courage to speak. When she finally did, her voice was hushed, as if even here, out in the open away from the eyes and ears of the town, she thought that someone would hear her.

"It started after the dust storm," she began. "I started to see things. Things no one should see."

"Like what?"

"Dr. Hudson. He had this… black fog around him when he visited daddy."

Penelope looked over at her sister, but Dynah stared out into the trees now, as if seeing it all over again. The road veered off through tall grasses up into the valley, and the horses headed home without any direction from the girls; they knew the way.

"Then, one day when I went to get water from the creek…" Dynah stopped speaking and shivered. "I could… feel the bodies in the graveyard calling to me."

Penelope took a moment to absorb what she'd heard. "I've definitely felt different ever since the dust storm," she finally admitted. "It seems when I get really angry that…"

Dynah's blue eyes burned into her. "That what?"

"That people get sick." Penelope shoulders shrunk in as she said it, as if she could protect herself from her sister's judgment.

"Like Daddy."

Penelope nodded slowly. "I wasn't trying to."

Dynah fell silent for so long that Penelope felt sure that her sister was angry, that her confession had driven an even larger wedge in between them. She hadn't thought it could get any wider.

"He's never treated you well," Dynah said at last.

Penelope's head jerked over to look at Dynah.

"I'm sorry I never said anything," Dynah added.

"You were just following our mother's example," Penelope

said softly. "I've been a constant reminder of her previous life, and I'm fairly certain she would erase all of that if she could. Including me."

Dynah winced. "I know it seems like that. But she loves you."

Penelope shrugged. "She's never done anything to show that she does."

They rode in silence for a half-mile, each in their own thoughts.

"It's not just us," Dynah said at last.

"Not just us?"

"Felicity, the merchant's daughter, she's been having strange things happen to her as well."

Penelope's eyes widened. "If she is, too, then that means—"

"Willow probably is."

"So, the dust storm, or the lightning, did... *something*... to all four of us."

The words hung in the air between them, lingering in the heat and the scent from the trees.

"What are we going to do?" Dynah asked.

"We need to get together. All four of us."

"Willow won't be back from the race until tomorrow."

Penelope nodded. "We finish the rodeo. Then we snag her as soon as she rides in."

Dynah worried her lower lip between her teeth. "Felicity and I saw a fortune teller that came in town for the rodeo. She said we were touched by evil and then she left town."

"My grandmother—Nascha—she said darkness had touched me," Penelope said. "I think we should all go see her. She won't turn us away."

Dynah's eyes sparked with what seemed to be hope. "That sounds like a good idea."

They rode the rest of the way back to the homestead discussing lighter subjects like the rodeo. When they got back, they each practiced with their horses, then bathed them and put them in stalls for the night with alfalfa hay. Finally, as the sky turned purple, they headed inside for dinner.

When Penelope finally got into bed for the night, she felt, for the first time in a very, very long time, that she actually had a sister.

The sun rose the next day in a blaze of promise. Penelope would compete in her first rodeo. They'd find Felicity and Willow and seek out answers to the strangeness that had taken over their lives. She'd be reunited with her clan.

Their mother was already up, making a hearty breakfast of biscuits and eggs and steak. The earthy smell of coffee boiling in the kettle made Penelope's stomach grumble. She sat down at the table as Dynah came bustling into the room, resplendent in one of her new blouses. She had something slung over her arm, which she tossed to Penelope.

"You'd look amazing in this lavender," she said. "I certainly don't need both of these new blouses."

"Thanks," Penelope said, feeling warmth spread through her chest.

Their mother turned and looked at them both, a question in her eyes, before setting the plates on the table in front of them. "I wish I didn't have to miss the rodeo." She wiped her hands on her apron. "But I don't think your father is feeling quite back to normal, and I can't just leave him here."

"It's okay, Mama," Dynah said.

Penelope just nodded. It didn't make any difference to her, and the comment hadn't been directed at her anyhow. Their mother grabbed her own plate of food and sat down with them, and the three of them ate in a comfortable silence. After they finished, Penelope and Dynah washed and dried the dishes.

"We'd better be getting on our way," Dynah said.

"I'll go change my shirt," Penelope said.

"I'll wait for you."

Penelope ducked into their room and quickly changed her old brown top for the crisp, new lavender one Dynah had gotten at the haberdashery a week ago. Her sister was right—it did look lovely against her cinnamon skin. She couldn't remember the last time she'd had a new blouse. She grabbed her chaps and her suede hat and headed back to the front of the house.

"Good luck," their mother said as Dynah opened the front door. "To both of you." And her eyes met Penelope's for the barest of moments.

Penelope, who had been halfway through the door, turned to her mother and smiled. That's when she saw Roy standing in the doorway to his bedroom.

A growl came from his throat. "I told you before, girl, you are *not* competing in that rodeo."

"Roy—" their mother began.

"Be quiet, woman," he said. "Do you think because I've been ill you all can do whatever you want? I'm still the head of this household."

He directed this last part to Penelope, his blue eyes daggers of ice.

"Daddy, don't overexert yourself," Dynah said, stepping back into the kitchen. "You're just starting to feel better."

"I don't need your mouth, either," he snarled. "Go out to the barn and get your horse. I'm going to have a *word* with Penelope."

Penelope could see her sister's eyes flicker with fear, and a tremble ran up her arms. "Go on, Dynah," she said quietly. "The rodeo needs its queen."

Dynah straightened. "No. I'm not going to the rodeo unless Penelope comes with me."

Roy's eyes bugged out of his head. "You'll do as I say. *Now!*"

"Come on, Pen," Dynah said, grabbing Penelope's hand.

They walked out of the house.

Penelope heard a roar like a bull behind them as Roy's temper exploded. Their steps quickened as they made their way around the side of the house toward the barn. Penelope felt her blood racing in her veins, her heart pounding in her jawline like a drum. They reached the barn and saddled the horses as quickly as they could. In less than five minutes they were back outside. Penelope swung into the saddle.

It was then that Roy came around the corner of the house, carrying his shotgun.

CHAPTER THIRTY-ONE

Felicity

A dusty arena certainly seemed no place for a grand piano. The crowd gathered for the start of the second day of the rodeo turned and stared as several men from the church helped heave the huge polished instrument out of the back of a wagon and onto the wooden stage at the head of the arena.

Morning sun peeked across the plains. Felicity turned from watching the men set up the piano and found herself looking around for Dynah. Her cheeks blushed, as if the people around her could read her thoughts. She shouldn't have given in to her feelings. They were wrong and she knew it. At least, that's what the church and her mother had always told her.

It had been a test, and clearly, she'd failed. At the first glimmer of attention from the Rodeo Queen, Felicity had fallen headfirst. And been rejected. Obviously Dynah liked men, as women were supposed to. Dynah also quite clearly no longer held interest in figuring out these strange things happening to them. In figuring out why electricity sparked between them when they touched, like a storm in their blood. Felicity had gone home that night, after the incident with the fortune teller, and she'd ripped out all the pages in her secret book in the barn and burned them inside a lantern. Watched each page curl and wither and die, consumed by flame.

No more dreaming of girls. No more fanciful thinking.

The first day of the rodeo had been a nice distraction. She'd played harp several times, both solo and with a group from church. The audience seemed to enjoy it, and she'd heard none of the usual whispered comments about the color of her skin or her family. It had been blissfully normal. Best yet, her mother still felt poorly so her father had allowed her to go alone, under the supervision of the preacher and his wife, of course.

Today, with the arrival of the piano, she and Travis would entertain the crowd with their duets, right up until the race riders started to come in, the grand finale of the hundred-mile race. The day before, everyone had waited eagerly as the messenger birds arrived, one by one, with each rider's position at the halfway point. Felicity had been surprised and secretly pleased that Willow, going by Will Bullet, had been in first place.

Travis appeared at her side, jolting her from her thoughts. "Want to do a practice run? Before the crowd gets even thicker?"

The rodeo started in another thirty minutes. Felicity nodded. "Good idea."

The piano now stood in the center of the stage, and she followed Travis up the steps at the back. They sat down at the piano, a respectable distance apart. Felicity shifted her cream-colored skirt and held her arms up over the keys. Tiny mother-of-pearl buttons ran down the sleeves at her wrists, and up her throat at the front. It was oppressively hot, so hot even the mosquitos weren't out.

"Ready?" she asked Travis.

He nodded and they began. They ran through several songs. They'd played so much together in the last week that they could pick up on a shift in tune from each other almost instantaneously. For fun, they went back and forth, changing songs to see if the other would miss a note. It had become somewhat of a game for them. They did it now, letting their fingers warm up, getting into the rhythm of the music. Travis looked over at her several times, grinning, and she found herself grinning right back.

After a few minutes, they stopped. Though it hadn't been an official performance, they still got a round of applause from those close by, and a few hoots and hollers of appreciation. Travis offered her his hand to help her off the piano bench, and then again when they descended the steps of the stage.

Felicity walked over to the church's covered wagon where

some of the women, including Abigail, were setting up a makeshift water station for the musicians. As Felicity approached, several of them clapped and smiled, and one of them handed her a tin cup of water. She drank thirstily, then walked around to the front of the wagon to check on Music where she stood hobbled with the wagon horses.

She and Travis weren't officially performing for another hour, so after patting Music and scratching the itchy spot under her mane, Felicity wandered over to the long avenue of traveling merchants. She'd wandered through once yesterday, but there were so many, dozens upon dozens, that she hadn't had a chance to take it all in.

As she strolled, she felt a tightness in her chest as she passed the empty spot where the fortune teller's tent had been. Felicity hurried past it, looking for something to distract her. She stepped into the tent of a purveyor of steam and clockwork mechanisms, everything from wind-up rabbits to clock-heart necklaces to steam-powered garden bed waterers.

After that she visited a hat shop and a saddlery and an herbologist. Near the end of the row, down toward the train station, an artist had set up an easel outside her tent. Felicity stopped to watch her work, and realized she was painting an angel. She stiffened, and her thoughts spun. She had the oddest feeling that she was forgetting something. A moment later the sensation passed.

"That's beautiful," she murmured.

The woman turned and smiled. She had deep auburn hair put up in a messy bun, and wore paint-splotched denim overalls with a red bandana around her neck. More like a farmer than a painter.

"Thank you. If you like angels, take a peek inside." And she swept her arm toward the open tent flaps.

Felicity ducked inside the tent. Her eyes widened. All of the paintings depicted angels. Or at first glance it seemed so—they were all beautiful, winged creatures. Wings of gold and wings of white. Gray and pale, pale blue like the first frost of winter. Wings in pastel sunset hues, pink and orange and purple. But when she looked further, she saw there were also beings with red wings, and wings black as night. Wings with storm clouds and universes in their depths. Angels with weapons in their hands, spears and flaming swords and golden bows. Felicity stared at these the longest. They made her heart beat faster, as if she gazed upon something forbidden.

When she finally emerged from the tent, the artist looked up at her. "What did you think?"

"Beautiful work," Felicity said politely. "Such diversity."

"They tend to focus on one type of angel in church," the painter said. "But there are so many." She paused, swiped a glob of paint across her canvas. "Or so I imagine."

"Are you much of a churchgoer yourself?" Felicity asked, her cheeks turning pink at the boldness of her question. She didn't know what kept coming over her lately.

The woman contemplated this a moment. "From time to time," she said softly. "I'm not much for blind faith. My truth comes from right here." And she placed her hand over her heart.

Felicity felt a thrill in her blood. And she'd thought *her* words stretched the boundaries of common courtesy. She realized she liked this woman who spoke her mind, who wasn't afraid.

"Well, I have to be getting back," Felicity said. "Thanks for talking to me."

The woman nodded and waved, paintbrush in hand.

Felicity headed back to the stage, suddenly worried she'd been gone too long. But a quick glance at her pocket watch told her she still had fifteen minutes. The crowd by the arena had nearly doubled since the rodeo had begun, and she had to skirt around the bulk of it to get back to the wagon. As she approached, she heard voices from the other side, though the covered top blocked her line of sight.

"Your son seems awfully friendly with the colored girl," said a woman's voice.

Felicity froze, except for her heart, which thrashed like a snared hawk in her chest. She didn't recognize the voice of the woman who said it. But the next voice she did recognize.

"No, they just play music together," said Abigail. "That's all it is."

"Well, I'd keep an eye on it if I were you. Rumors will fly faster than those race riders if you don't."

The preacher's wife cleared her throat. "No need for concern. She's a nice girl, and a great musician, but it's out of the question. Travis is a smart boy. He knows these things. He'll marry someone… *appropriate.*"

It shattered then, Felicity's fragile happiness, like a piece of blown glass. She'd thought she belonged somewhere, finally, found a group that looked past the color of her skin. But they had rejected her, too. Like her mother rejected her. Like Dynah rejected her. And now the preacher's wife, the one she trusted the most.

The lightning surged inside of her. The magic. That's what it was, there was no use denying it anymore. The fortune teller had called it by its name. Felicity had no need to sidestep the truth any longer.

Her hands began to glow, and she made no attempt to hide it. She felt… angry. No, far too mild a word. Like comparing a summer rain shower to a typhoon. *Enraged.* That described how she truly felt. No matter what she did or how perfectly she behaved, it was never good enough, not for anyone.

Felicity's fury and sorrow ballooned inside of her. And it was in that moment she felt the call. *Her* call. She recognized it instantly, realized a part of her had been waiting for it, ever since the dust storm.

She strode to Music, swung up into the saddle, and galloped away from the arena.

CHAPTER THIRTY-TWO

Dynah

Dynah's father lifted his shotgun and pointed it at Penelope and Domino.

Everything fractured into milliseconds, each containing a frozen image, a frozen drop of time. Her father's face, twisted in rage, as he sighted down the length of the gun. Penelope yanking the reins to spin Domino. Their mother, screaming, lunging for his arm.

The gun fired. A blossom of red-orange-gold as the bullet left the barrel. A sound loud enough to tear the sky.

Domino screamed and staggered. A spot of red blossomed on his hindquarters. Dynah thought she'd been grazed by buckshot, too. Everything went vivid red and hazy. Penelope screamed, and Dynah couldn't tell if it was pain or rage or both.

Her mother hung from her father's shoulder; it was the only

reason he'd missed a direct shot. He elbowed her in the face and she hit the ground hard. An inarticulate sound rose out of him, like a wounded animal. He leveled his weapon and fired again.

This time the shot didn't go wide. It flew straight and true. And her mother leapt up, directly in front of it.

Dynah's vision pulsed, a heartbeat, red and bloody.

Her mother's body lying on the ground…

A stain spreading across her breast, spilling across the ground…

Her father stepping forward, standing over the body, his gun lifting again...

Boom. Boom. Boom. Dynah's blood pulsed within her. The world pounded around her. Her fury spread its wings, and blackness overcame the red.

Then *she* was the pulse. A single pulse, a flash of darkness. The power inside of her lashed out, and her father's body joined her mother's in the dirt.

And she became the blackness, and it consumed everything. Burned through her, burned everything around her. Raged, a storm without boundaries. Desolated, decimated, drowned, smothered.

Until she brushed up against another force.

Her sister. Or rather, her sister's pain. Her torment, her fury.

Dynah opened her eyes. Penelope stood a few feet away, trying to stop the blood pouring from Domino's hindquarters. Tears streamed down her face, but they were black, like runnels of ink. She could feel the power coming off her, that same lightning that had touched them both.

Their eyes met, and they could see each other's thoughts. Dynah stepped closer and clasped Penelope's fingers, then they raised their hands together to the sky. The power intensified, as if it had been waiting for this moment, for them to join together. A bolt of lightning shot down and enveloped Domino's body.

It looked for a moment as if he were melting. Or rather, the shedding of a cloak, a snake releasing its skin. A *transformation*. The lightning moved into him and became him. And when it ceased a moment later, he stood there, pure white. Lightning incarnate.

"I dreamed of this," Penelope murmured.

"So did I," Dynah said.

They looked at each other, then over to the body of their mother, and Dynah's father. Nothing much remained of them now. Dynah's magic had turned everything on the homestead to black ash and rot, as if ten thousand years had passed in a handful of moments.

"Are you sad?" Penelope asked her. Her voice sounded detached, a million miles away.

Dynah didn't answer for a moment. "I'm not sure what I am anymore."

The words had barely left her mouth when she felt it, and the way Penelope's head whipped around, she could tell her sister felt it, too. A call. A call they had to answer.

Boom. Boom. Boom.

The world pulsed around her again.

Penelope swung up onto the pure white horse, and Dynah mounted Moon. They rode west.

CHAPTER THIRTY-THREE

Willow

The rain had long since washed them clean of the mud, and they'd mounted back up and ridden for the mountains under the light of the moon. With Zane by her side, Willow had one more set of eyes to watch for traps and ambushes. Though they hadn't seen any other riders in hours.

Around midnight they found a spot to rest near a creek in one of the canyons. No trees overhanging for mountain lions to leap down from, plenty of visibility to see if any of the competition tried to sneak up on them. They made sure the horses drank their fill, then they moved a bit away from the water to avoid incidents with wild animals visiting for a drink in the middle of the night.

Willow picked a place with some grass for Bullet to eat and took off her saddle and bridle. Then she laid down next to her.

Zane flopped down beside them and pulled Willow into his arms before dusting her lips with a kiss and beginning to snore. Willow fell fast asleep a few moments later. It had been an arduous day to say the least.

A few hours later, she awoke just before the sun emerged. She'd always woken right before dawn, even as a young child. As if she could feel the light birthing each new day. The earth awakening from darkness, life blinking its eyes, hushed perfection, unbroken by the cruelties that often came later.

She was alone.

Willow blinked and sat up. Bullet stood sleeping a couple feet away from her, her breath deep and sonorous, nostrils flaring in and out slowly. She looked black in the deep gray of first dawn. Jericho wasn't there, either.

And just as her heart started pounding in her chest, Zane walked up from the creek, leading his horse. "Morning, angel," he said, and he handed her a single yellow daisy.

She took it from him and smiled. She'd never been given a flower by a boy before. They'd always been too scared to approach her. Guns were more her style, but Willow thought it was a sweet gesture. A strange fluttering filled her chest.

"We should be about ten miles from the northern checkpoint." She got up and put her hat on, then tucked the daisy inside the pocket on the breast of her shirt.

"That sounds about right," Zane said.

They shared a breakfast of dried jerky and saddled the horses back up. Then they continued through the canyons toward the checkpoint.

A couple hours later they reached it. Like the first checkpoint, it was just a wagon sitting in the middle of nowhere with two cowboys and a stock of messenger birds. Willow and Zane made sure to ride in a ways apart to make it less obvious they were together. Zane nodded for her to go ahead of him.

"Will Bullet," said one of the cowboys as he wrote the name down on a piece of paper. He whistled and eyed her up and down, clearly surprised. "You're still in the lead, kid."

Willow refrained from making a face at the use of the term *kid* and simply nodded, suppressing her elation. The other cowboy stuck a piece of paper with her alias on it inside a hawk's mouth, wound up the clockwork, and sent it flying off into the sky. Willow urged Bullet into a lope and continued on down the mountain pass until she was out of sight, then stopped to wait for Zane.

Just thirty miles left to go. The final stretch.

She heard hoofbeats behind her and quickly realized it was more than one set. More like several. Zane came into view with five other riders behind him. Willow wasn't sure what to do for a moment. Should she wait for Zane, making it obvious they had an alliance, or should she ride out ahead? After several moments of internal conflict, Bullet prancing and snorting between her, she decided to wait. If she galloped off now, she'd spend a good deal of Bullet's energy, and she couldn't sustain that for thirty miles. She just needed to stay within striking distance for the final gallop into Hawk's Hollow. Plus, she didn't want Zane to think she was ditching him.

"We caught 'im, boys!" hollered one of the men to the others.

The group galloped up and surrounded her and Bullet, milling around like hunting dogs sniffing our their prey.

"Thought yuh'd stay in the lead the 'ole race, eh?" said another, spitting tobacco on the ground.

"Glad to finally have some competition," Willow said with a smile. "May the best man win." And she tipped her hat to them.

"The best man," Zane said. "Or *woman.*"

Willow froze and looked at him, staring into those river-blue eyes. He ripped his gaze away from her. The other cowboys looked confused.

"Woman?" snorted one of them.

Zane tipped his hat in her direction. Five sets of eyes landed on her face, the bullseye of a shooting target. The blood drained from Willow's body.

"Yuh sayin' this here is a woman?" asked one of the men dubiously.

"Dun't look like no woman," said another.

"Oh, I *assure* you she is," Zane said with a smirk that left no doubt as to his meaning. And this time he did look at her, just for a moment, and his eyes and his smile ripped into her like a rock salt shot.

"Hoo-wee!" yelled a couple of the men.

"You givin' out more freebies, darlin'?"

"Fast and loose, just like I like 'em."

It surged out of her then, the lightning and the rage, so hot it was white. Her fury rolled across them all like a thundercloud. The laughter of the men died, and they all pulled out their guns. A half-moment of tension and confusion shimmered between them as they tried to comprehend what was happening to them. Then bullets flew back and forth, a hail of metal. The storm coming off Willow protected her and her mare. They existed as pure energy now, pure power. Blood spattered, screams flew from lips, men fell from their horses.

And her anger wasn't spent. Not even close. Willow had an ocean of wrath inside of her and it shot out through the canyon, over the earth, up into the sky. She knew then what had happened to her, to them, that day in the cyclone. The magic told her, showed her their purpose. And a *great* purpose it was. She issued a call to her sisters, her fellow Riders.

Willow took one last look at Zane's lifeless body, lying amidst the others, as she plucked the daisy from her pocket, dropped it on his chest. Then she pressed her legs to Bullet's sides and shot forward to the east.

It had begun.

CHAPTER THIRTY-FOUR

Death and Pestilence and Famine joined up in the plains like magnets drawn together, then they continued west following War's call.

When the four Riders met, magic pulsed across the desert. They became something different. Something more. Like moths escaping their chrysalises, they came into their highest forms, they claimed the fullness of their power, they *transformed*.

A glow surrounded them and it rose into the sky, creating a storm of heat and raw energy. Dark clouds rolled in from all directions, spinning overhead, and a wind rushed in from the north. The ground cracked beneath the hooves of their horses and the screams of demons rent the air.

And then they rode.

East, towards the little town of Hawk's Hollow, a town of

farmers and a town of merchants, a town with a lazy creek meandering through it, a town nestled beneath the shadows of red mountain peaks. The town where it all began. The town where it all would end.

The Riders galloped, four in a row.

Pestilence on her pure white horse, bleaching the color from the earth and the heavens as she passed.

War on her red horse, flames shooting out behind them into the sky.

Famine on her black horse, leaving a wake of universe behind her, a rip in time and space.

Death on her pale horse, calling forth an army of the dead; men and women and beasts.

Angels and demons alike watched as the apocalypse began. But the townsfolk of Hawk's Hollow knew not what rode toward them.

On the horizon, the spire of the church came into view.

CHAPTER THIRTY-FIVE

War

War galloped through the crowds gathered around the arena, and up Main Street through the center of town. Where she passed, people began to argue, to throw punches, to pull weapons.

They had all held her back. The *world* had held her back. Too opinionated, too brash, too emotional. She'd built a wall against it, a wall to protect her heart, her soul. But still someone had slipped past her defenses. Claimed to care for her while spinning lies. No more. She had been weak before, but now she'd grown *strong*. She'd show them all. Her place was everywhere and everything she wanted it to be.

After making one loop through Hawk's Hollow, she pulled her flaming horse to a halt in front of a group of brawling cowboys. They stopped their violence and looked up at her, entranced.

"Ride forth," War called, "To all corners of the land. Sow your discord, your hatred, your viciousness. Cross the oceans, climb mountains. Do not stop until every inch of the earth knows my message."

And they mounted their horses, and they turned from each other, and they each galloped off in a different direction.

CHAPTER THIRTY-SIX

Pestilence

Pestilence rode to the river and raised a bow, notched it with a poisoned arrow. She shot it into the flowing water, which turned from crystal clear to a murky green. Next, she shot an arrow to the sky and issued a pulse of power. The air grew thick and noxious and spread outward across the plains and over the mountains.

Poison and disease, the same she'd felt living inside her every day of her life. Different than the rest, treated like some sort of lesser being. Constantly degraded, until she had believed it herself. Now *all* could feel that selfsame torture.

She rode next to the train station, and as she galloped past the train stopped there, she fired an arrow into each cargo carriage. Then, with a jolt of magic, she sent the train moving down the tracks toward Denver.

Airships came next, she summoned them forth from their journeys across the sky and she infected each and every one of them, then sent them forth again to travel the land.

CHAPTER THIRTY-SEVEN

Famine

Famine rode from field to field, orchard to orchard. Fields of wheat and beans and berries. Orchards of apples and peaches and cherries. At each she paused, raised her scales of justice, and shriveled the green things that grew there, the things that brought nourishment and life.

She had known hunger, *oh* but had she known hunger. To want and want and want, and never receive. To feel an emptiness inside that could never be filled, a vast chasm, a darkness like the rips she left behind her as she rode. They would all feel the pain that she had felt, the desperate longing for fulfillment.

She ruined the soil, too, so that nothing could grow there again. Cast her magic far, felt it burrow through the earth, spreading from tree to tree. On and on and on until the world was as empty as she was.

CHAPTER THIRTY-EIGHT

Death

Death sat on her pale horse south of town and watched it all unfold.

All her life she'd thought she had control, had the upper hand. It had all been a lie. She'd been nothing but an object to them all, a pretty face and nothing more, a tool at their disposal. And now, as she watched it all crumble, she smiled.

Behind her, a mass of writhing skeletons stood, awaiting her command. Men, women, children. Those that had been white, and black, and native. Color didn't matter when you were dead; we are all the same in the end. Hundreds upon hundreds of them, and more coming. Those who had fallen in the hundreds and thousands of years before. From sickness or battle or old age. And not just people, but animals, too. Bears and mountain lions and wolves and deer and eagles.

She heard it then, the call of something from another time, something *ancient*. Trapped beneath the earth, under layers and layers of sediment and rock. Death turned to the north and raised a hand, sent forth her dark magic. Cleared a path, increased the strength of her call.

Even from miles away, she could hear the top of the mountain explode. Her blood thrilled in her veins as it came toward her, closer and closer and closer.

It screamed as it flew over Hawk's Hollow, a cry that shattered the sky, a sound that shivered the souls of everyone who heard it. It circled once over the town, and then the bone dragon landed at the feet of its mistress with a resounding boom.

CHAPTER THIRTY-NINE

The dragon acted as a beacon, and the four Riders gathered together and watched the chaos they had wrought.

"What next?" Famine asked, and they all looked to War.

"Next we do what we do best: we ride." She was beautiful and terrifying to behold, lit from within by her fury. "This place is just the beginning."

The air shimmered around them, then, and there came the sound of wings.

A host of angels stood before them, a couple dozen at least. At the center stood an angel with pale skin and golden wings. He smiled beatifically and spread his arms in a gesture of welcome.

"Well done, Riders," said the angel, his words wrapping

around them like velvet. "You are true warriors of Heaven. Here, today, you have initiated a vital cleansing of the earth. A cleansing of souls."

The Riders looked at each other, and at the angels. They could share thoughts now, so they conversed without words.

"He's not lying," said Pestilence. "Our magic feels the same as their magic. We are *from* them."

Confusion pulsed off of War. "From Heaven? From angels?" Something inside of her flickered, some emotion from the woman she had been.

"This is our purpose," Death intoned. "The Apocalypse. A new beginning."

Famine had gone still, her head cocked to the side. "Something isn't right… I remember…"

But the angel spoke again before her mind could settle on the thought.

"I am Alinar," he said, and his silver halo pulsed with a bright light.

"What would you have us do, Alinar?" asked War. Her flaming mount pawed one hoof at the ground beneath them.

The angel spread his arms wide to indicate the destruction around them. "You have already begun. Now you ride forth, in Heaven's name."

The four Riders eyed the angels. Famine startled as she recognized two of the angels as the thieves from her stable. Pestilence saw a beautiful, black-haired angel, the woman who had paid her entry at the rodeo. Death saw several faces familiar to her, though they looked completely transformed now, the men who had harassed her at the arena. And War recognized one in particular.

Eyes the blue of a river, hair of deepest night.

"Evolution is a messy business, I'm afraid," Alinar continued. "We stand before you to congratulate you on your birth to a higher form. It was necessary to push you through darkness before you could reach the light." He nodded to the angels on each side of him. "But now we can all join together in this battle for the souls of mankind."

War ripped her eyes from the angel who had crushed her heart. "Mankind?" she echoed. "In Heaven's name?"

A ripple of movement stirred the angels.

"Of course," Alinar said, his halo pulsing again. "Heaven granted you these powers, so it is for Heaven you will use them."

"I remember now," Famine whispered in the minds of the other three.

She remembered the girl she had been, the girl who had suffered so, the girl who prayed dutifully every day and attended every church service without fail. And she remembered the winged being from the church, the words he had spoken. The being she had thought was an angel.

But he wasn't here before them now.

The other Riders watched her thoughts, her memories, and

together they listened to the words from the church that day.

"What I'm about to tell you will be vital in the coming days," said the winged being. "But I'm afraid you won't remember this conversation, not until you need to. Now hear my words…"

He paused.

"Heaven and Hell have been locked in battle for eternity, a battle for souls. The Apocalypse is Heaven's way of tipping the scales in their favor. A reaping of souls. A cleansing, they will call it. Necessary for the survival of humanity, they'll say."

"But aren't you an angel?" Felicity asked.

"What I am is not important." The being shook his head. "What you must remember, when the time comes, is this: you have a choice. Heaven does not control you. No one controls you. Humanity, good and bad, messy and beautiful, terrible and wonderful, with all its flaws and imperfections, is worth saving."

And then, with a sound of wings, the being was gone.

The Riders watched all of this inside Famine's head in the blink of an eye.

Each of them remembered, for just the most fleeting of moments, their own humanity. Pestilence remembered her clan, a white wolf, sage smoke beneath the moon. Death remembered a cool breeze over her skin, patting her horse's sweaty shoulder after a hard ride. War remembered the wonder of the dragonflies in the gun shop, the whir of their wings and the tick-tick-tick as they counted time. And Famine remembered the feel of thick pages beneath her fingers, the smell of ink and hay and sunshine.

There was pain, too, and loss, and soul-splitting agony. But their choice was made.

"Are you ready, then?" Alinar said. "To continue the grand mission you have begun? To explore the full potential of your power?"

War stepped forward, flames flaring around her. "It seems to us that Heaven is only interested in using us, just as we've been used by everyone else in our lives."

And everything froze. Quite literally.

Alinar, brow furrowed, arm raised in the air. The other angels, varying expressions of disbelief and anger on their faces. The town behind them, that moments before had been a writhing nest of chaos, smoke, and fire.

A new being materialized before them. Brown skin, silver hair, red wings. He gazed on them with golden eyes, and Famine gasped.

"You!"

The other Riders recognized him from her memory. The being from the church.

"I prayed that you would make this choice," the being said, and he bowed his head to them. "I am only here because you did."

Famine pointed at him. "But in the church that day, your wings were golden!"

"A necessary deceit," he said apologetically.

"We've been seeing a lot of that lately," War growled, and the earth rumbled beneath her feet.

"What exactly are you?" Pestilence said, raising her bow and pointing it at him.

Death gazed upon him stoically. "A demon, by the looks of it."

"Exactly why I disguised the color of my wings that day," the being said. "I am neither angel nor demon, or perhaps you could say I am both. I am Fallen."

"Fallen?" Famine questioned.

"I reject the authority of both Heaven and Hell," he said. "I am here because there are those of us who wish to save humanity, not cleanse it. You can call me Beziel."

CHAPTER FORTY

So, Beziel," Death said, "What is it the Fallen want from us?"

He fell silent for several moments. "Before I can answer that, you must know the history behind all of this. You know of the battle between Heaven and Hell, the battle that has raged for eternity." The sadness in his eyes felt palpable. "They've tried to start this war before, with other Riders, Riders who come from Heaven itself. But this time they used humans. Because who better to destroy the earth than its own inhabitants? You, shall we say, know the territory?"

The Riders cast each other glances. "Go on," said War.

"The angels, as is typical of their kind, bound you in a magical contract without telling you they were doing it," Beziel said. "But a contract isn't truly valid unless both parties agree to it."

"Meaning, we can still say no," Famine said.

"But what would happen if we do that?" Death asked.

Pestilence's eyes flashed. "Would we have to give up this power?"

Their thoughts flickered and merged between them. They couldn't go back. Not now. Not after everything they had been through. The earth began to shake beneath them as their anger surged.

Beziel raised his hands in a placating gesture. "That's not actually what we want you to do."

Four sets of eyes locked onto the Fallen, and even at his age, older than time itself, he felt the power behind that collective gaze, and it made him flinch deep inside.

"We want you to keep your powers," Beziel said. "*Need* you to keep them. We just want you to use them for our side. To stop both Heaven and Hell. But without letting them know you're working for us." His eyes roved over each of them in turn. "Double agents."

"Double agents?" Famine echoed.

The Riders each looked at each other, unspoken words passing between them.

"There are conditions," War said.

"Of course," Beziel said. "State them."

"We don't want to work for *your side*, or any side. Our time of being used by others is over. But," and she gazed on him with flame-filled eyes, "It appears our goals may align at the moment. We don't want to destroy *everything*."

And that part of each of them that was now more than human flared. With the magic had come knowledge, a vast knowledge that spanned all of time. They knew *so much*. So much more than their short human lives. It was as if the magic was another being living inside them. They saw the span of human history pass before their eyes, and fury rose within them. Some suffering was due. Some vengeance. Many wrongs had been done, and justice had to be served.

"I can see your struggle," Beziel said, his golden eyes glowing softly. "Your *darkness*. You possessed it as humans, as all humans do, and now it is so much more. *You* are so much more. But hope also lives within you. Joy. Love. You must battle to find a balance within, or the battle out there—" he waved his arm across the sky— "is already lost."

The Riders thought on this. On their lives before. On their transformation. On the things they had already done. Reality was already unraveling beneath their fingertips…

"I don't know how we can possibly undo this damage," Pestilence said, and a shiver of horror ran through her.

"The Apocalypse has already begun," Death said. "Can we even stop it now?"

"No," Beziel said. "You can't. Not yet, or else Heaven and Hell will realize you've changed sides."

Famine cocked her head to the side. "You want us to… let

the Apocalypse happen?"

The Fallen's wings flared out behind him. "In order to win this war, once and for all, there's only one thing that can be done. I'm not saying I want you to let the Apocalypse happen."

He paused, pulled on the reserves of strength within him to utter the unspeakable.

"I'm saying you must first make the Apocalypse worse."

The Riders stared at him.

"Now," said Beziel, "Listen very carefully. Here's what you need to do next."

THE END

ACKNOWLEDGEMENTS

A huge thank you to Marsha Hartford Sapp, the most badass horsewoman I know. Thanks for being an awesome trainer and friend all these years. Max and I wouldn't have made it this far without you. And for the fog machine!

I'm so grateful to Ash Mancuso, incredible horsewoman, filmmaker, and yoga instructor. I had no idea what a transformative creative journey making the book trailer would be, and you were a stellar guide and friend every step of the way.

For all the other women at Southern Oaks Equestrian Center. My horsewomen. My posse. You know who you are.

So much thanks to Solange Charles and Elroy Keetso for editing and helping me get Felicity and Penelope right. To Matt, for his dope editing skills and being the eternal cheerleader. Also to my wonderful critique partners Don, Nancy, and Melissa for their awesome edits. And a big thanks to Reginah WaterSpirit for warm-heartedly connecting me with so many people in the Navajo community.

And of course for Max, the pale horse of my heart. A little piece of my soul goes into each book I create, but the biggest piece lives inside of this equine. Way too clever and handsome for his own good, and he knows it.

Books by A.A. Chamberlynn

Of Blood, Earth, and Magic

The Four Horsewomen Series

A War of Daisies (Book 1)
A Death of Music (Book 2)
A Famine of Crows (Book 3)
A Pestilence of Pride (Book 4)

The Zyan Star Series

Martinis with the Devil (Book 1)
Whiskey and Angelfire (Book 2)
Vengeance and Vermouth (Book 3)
Black Magic and Mojitos (Prequel Novelette)
Sorcery and Sidecars (Origin Story Novella)

The Quinn Chronicles
(A Zyan Star Spin-off Series)

Death and Dating (Book 1)
Death and Promises (Book 2)
Death and Eternity (Book 3)

The Timekeeper's War Series

Huntress Found (Book 1)
Huntress Lost (Book 2)
Huntress at War (Book 3)

www.AlexiaChamberlynn.com

GET A FREE BOOK!

Subscribe to Alexia's newsletter at
www.alexiachamberlynn.com

Subscribers get access to book giveaways and
advanced reading copies.

WANT TO BE AN AUTHOR'S BEST FRIEND?

Blood, sweat, tears, wine, and a little piece of my soul went into writing this book. I'd love to know what you think! Leave a review on Goodreads and your book retailer of choice. Tell me your favorite character or your favorite scene. Reviews help authors a ton, both in ranking algorithms and making a living, so I much appreciate it!

You can also email me a note or send fan art (I LOVE fan art!) to alexiachamberlynn@gmail.com or come chat with me on Facebook, Instagram, or BookBub!

www.alexiachamberlynn.com

ABOUT THE AUTHOR

Alexia writes novels about magic, adventure, and romance. She lives in Florida with her son and a menagerie of animals. When she's not writing or reading, she can be found playing with horses, drinking wine, traveling to the next place on her global wish list, or maybe doing yoga. Dr. Who, unicorns, and katanas make her very happy.

www.ingramcontent.com/pod-product-compliance
Lightning Source LLC
Chambersburg PA
CBHW020909160726
47993CB00005B/1882